What girls like you are saying...

"I loved it! I wanted to keep reading till the end. I was definitely hooked into this book. When the chapters ended, it made me want to read the next chapter, it was so exciting! I totally wanted to find out what happened. I loved the book. I think it should be published right away. If it doesn't get published I'll tear my hair out!" Piper, age 10

"This is the best book ever! Yes, I would be interested in reading more Katie Carlson stories!" Sarah, age 10

"I loved the book. I liked that Katie learned to know God and how to be a good example and that it was about horses. Thanks for letting me read the book, it was fun!" Jessica, age 10

"*Adventure at Cassidy Ranch* was fun and exciting! I liked how everything came together in the end." Kelsey, age 11

"I liked that I really learned about God's Word more and what it really means to me. It taught me in a way that was easy to learn. I felt it was made just for me. I think it would be great for girls my age, younger or older. I like the chapter length—they end right at a good part, making you want to read more. YES! YES! YES, I would read more Katie Carlson stories because I want to know what happens to her. It would be really cool if you could make a really long series." Molly, age 12

"I liked the Christian perspective, it had good interesting characters, and it was exciting." Erin, age 12

ADVENTURE AT CASSIDY RANCH

Judy Starr

Dolphin Bay Publishing

Adventure at Cassidy Ranch

Published by:
Dolphin Bay Publishing, Inc.
P.O. Box 3664
Dana Point, CA 92629
www.katiecarlsonbooks.com

ISBN 978-0-9899230-0-2

Dedication:

This Katie Carlson book series is dedicated to my precious
Mom
who taught me all about adventure and fun,

and to my amazing husband,
Stottler
who brings adventure and fun into my life every single day.

Chapter 1

Katie lay on her stomach across her bed, a bright green flip-flop dangling from her toe, and her favorite horse story propped up against the pillows. She glanced over at her prized horse statues lined up near her dresser. It looked like they were prancing across the pink carpet. She couldn't help smiling as she pictured herself galloping on a powerful stallion through a prairie of tall green grass. *I wish I could have a horse!* she thought, a familiar daydream repeated many times a day.

"Dave! Mark! Katie!" her mother's voice echoed down the hall. "Dinner—it's lasagna. Wash your hands."

Lasagna! Katie leaped off her bed, sending the paperback flying. She quickly bent down to pick it up, and once more the picture on the cover caught her attention. Large trees and a red-roofed barn formed the background, but it was the beautiful, dark chestnut stallion looking out at her with enormous brown eyes that made her heart feel like it was being squeezed in her chest. "He's perfect," she sighed, reaching a finger out to touch the horse's nose.

Suddenly her hand froze. Katie stared hard at the cover illustration. Were the trees and barn actually…*growing?* "Am I getting sick?" she said as she turned around and tried to grab her desk to steady herself. But for some reason, the desktop seemed out of reach.

Katie squeezed her eyes tight, then slowly opened them again. Instantly her heart began to race, because now *everything* in her room looked tiny and far away, as if she was peering through the wrong end of a pair of binoculars. *What's happening to me?*

Katie's room continued shrinking before her eyes, then disappeared altogether! Suddenly she found herself somehow suspended in the air, looking down on her house. She thought she saw a large man standing in her front yard, smiling up at her, but she couldn't be sure. All she knew was that her whole body was now starting to spin, like a bug being wound in a spider's web. It made her awfully dizzy, and she had a weird thought that her eyes might be whirling around like two clock hands twirling in opposite directions. "Ohhhhhh…" she moaned as she clamped her eyes tightly shut again.

The next thing she knew, she'd landed with a hard thump on her backside. Her eyes popped open with the jolt, and her heart pounded in her ears. Shaking her head slightly, she struggled to see through her dizziness. *Where am I?* she wondered, feeling powdery dirt beneath her hands.

As her head began to clear, Katie realized she was sitting on the ground, her back leaning up against a rough wooden fence. A warm jet of air from above ruffled her hair. She glanced upward—and found herself nose to nose with a long, brown, curious face. *A horse!*

Dust scattered from her shorts as she grabbed the wooden railing and stood up on shaky legs. *Is he real?* she wondered, reaching out toward the horse's forelock. *What just happened? Where—?*

"Do you like to play in the dirt?" The sudden voice from behind startled her.

Whirling around, Katie squinted into the bright sunlight. Not far away stood a boy, his hands shoved deep inside faded jeans' pockets. She thought he must be about her age. She saw his green eyes studying her from beneath his mop of red hair that shone like fire in the afternoon sun.

"Huh?" Katie asked in confusion. She looked around quickly, trying to make sense of all this. *Trees, a red-roofed barn, a chestnut-colored horse.* Then her heart felt like it almost stopped. *I'm inside the book!*

Hesitantly the boy began to walk toward her, a puzzled grin across his freckled face. Dust rose in puffs around his cowboy boots as he came a few steps closer.

Katie met his eyes. "Is…is all this…r-r-real?" she stammered.

In response, he moved closer and said, "Does this feel real?" On purpose he stepped on her sandaled toes with his boot.

3

"Oww!" she hollered, instantly giving his shoulder an emphatic whack.

The boy quickly raised his fists, but before a real scuffle could start, a voice from the barn called, "Zack!"

Katie and the boy both turned toward a tall man walking swiftly toward them. He was wearing a plaid shirt, jeans, boots, and a large tan cowboy hat. In a stern voice he said, "Fighting is not allowed on this ranch. You know that, Zack."

"Yes, sir," the boy said, lowering his arms slightly, but keeping a stare fixed on Katie.

When the lanky man reached them, his face softened a bit as he turned toward Katie. "We've been looking for you," he said.

Katie felt her eyes grow wide. "You have?"

He nodded. "You're the girl that came with the horse we just bought, right?"

Now she was *really* confused. "Uh, horse?"

The tall man gestured toward the animal behind her. "Tango. You know—the Quarter Horse, right there beside you," he said, sounding perplexed.

Katie turned to look at the horse that had startled her moments ago. His dark eyes surveyed her curiously, and a gentle breeze brushed his reddish-brown mane against his muscular neck. Without even thinking, she immediately reached out to stroke his face. "He's gorgeous!"

As she continued to pat the horse, the rancher moved up next to her. "The man who sold Tango to us said he'd recently been used as a cutting horse," he said to Katie. "But the gentleman also told us that Tango is very special, because he comes with a girl who will calm him down. That's obviously you—so he's all yours for now."

Katie could hardly believe her ears. *He's mine? I've begged for a horse all my life, and now this incredible horse is mine?* She began bouncing up and down a little on her toes. *I'm actually on the ranch in my favorite book, and I have a horse! This is too good to be true!* As her mind raced to grasp all that was happening, she couldn't think of anything to say.

Zack broke in. "Cat got your tongue? Looks like you've seen a ghost." He turned toward the cowboy. "Hey, Dad, maybe she's not the right girl. Uh, she looks like she's not all here, if you know what I mean," he said, rolling his eyes.

Katie didn't understand all that was going on, but she definitely knew when she'd been insulted. "If it looks like I've seen a ghost, it's because I'm looking at *you!*" she snapped.

But before Katie and Zack could start in again, the man said quickly, "Well, it looks like you two have met. But I don't know your name yet." He held out a calloused hand. "I'm Matthew Cassidy, Zack's father."

"I'm Katie Carlson," she said, turning abruptly away from the annoying boy and reaching out gingerly to shake the man's leathery hand. His kind hazel eyes immediately made her feel welcome.

"Well, Katie," he said, releasing her hand, "we're awfully glad you've come to live with us for a while."

You have no idea, Katie thought. She couldn't stop the enormous smile spreading across her face. She glanced over at the obnoxious kid. Even *he* couldn't spoil the joy of living on a real ranch with her own horse.

Mr. Cassidy motioned toward the dirt road leading up to the ranch house. "Let's go introduce you to Mrs. Cassidy and Anna," he said as he began to walk. "Then you can get settled in."

Settled in, Katie repeated to herself as she trotted a few steps to catch up with Mr. Cassidy. *I wonder if I get to stay here for a long time. I hope so—this is what I've always dreamed of!*

Katie eagerly took in everything around her. They passed a simple wooden bunkhouse on their right as they drew close to the Cassidy's single-story adobe ranch home. *This is amazing,* she thought. The huge grin across her face felt like it might just remain there permanently.

Zack had been following closely behind, but soon moved up alongside her. Out of the corner of her eye she saw him take a big breath and stand as tall as possible. "I'm twelve," he announced.

Katie glared over at him. "Well, so am I."

"Oh," Zack said, his shoulders dropping slightly. "Uh… well my hair is way redder than yours."

"My hair is *auburn,* you doofus," she said, flipping it back from her face and wishing she'd been able to bring along a scrunchy to hold it back.

Mr. Cassidy's voice got Katie's attention away from the pest beside her. "So, Katie," he said over his shoulder, "how do you like Northern Colorado? The fellow who sold Tango to us said you'd feel right at home here."

6

Katie's mind spun. *Just a minute ago I was lying on my bed in our house in Oklahoma, and now I'm in Colorado. It doesn't make any sense—but I don't care.* "I *love* it here!" she practically shouted. "This is perfect!" Glancing over at Zack, she thought about adding, *except for him,* but she decided to leave that part out for now.

When they reached the side door of the ranch house, Mr. Cassidy and Zack immediately removed their boots and placed them on a rack beside the door. Mr. Cassidy turned to meet her puzzled eyes and said, "Wouldn't want to track anything that's on the bottom of these into the house, would we?"

Katie nodded and started to kick off her sandals as well. But before she could add them to the rack, the air was shattered by a child's scream!

Chapter 2

Like lightning, Matthew Cassidy flung open the door and bolted into the house, Zack close on his heels. Katie froze, wondering what she should do, then hurriedly decided to follow them inside.

As Katie stepped into the hallway, she heard lots of voices toward her right. She hesitantly walked in that direction, and quickly came to a living room buzzing with frantic activity. Katie saw Mr. Cassidy and a woman bent over something hidden from view behind a large oak coffee table. Beside them, Zack was righting an overturned wheelchair.

"Are you okay, sweetheart?" Mr. Cassidy was saying, scooping up a pale little girl into his arms.

"I'm all right, Daddy," the girl replied in a small voice as she wrapped her arms tightly around his neck.

Zack turned to look at the woman. "What happened, Mom?"

"I'm fine," the girl put in. "I reached over and lost my balance, that's all." The pink flush in her cheeks grew as she added, "It just surprised me."

The woman tenderly smoothed the child's long blonde hair. "You're sure you're okay, sweetie?" she asked.

"I'm fine, Mama. Really I am," came her soft answer.

Katie shifted uncomfortably from one foot to the other as she observed the scene before her. She felt like she had intruded on a private family matter, and now she didn't know how to back away without being noticed.

As if he could read her mind from across the room, Mr. Cassidy suddenly turned to her and said, "Oh! Katie, come on in here."

Katie hesitantly took several steps into the room while Mr. Cassidy gently set the girl in the wheelchair. Then he addressed the woman. "Honey, I'd like you to meet Katie Carlson." Turning toward Katie he said, "This is my wife, Susan Cassidy."

Katie looked at the beautiful lady. Her smile seemed to light up the entire room. Katie took a step toward her and held out her hand a little ways, which was instantly captured in Mrs. Cassidy's warm handshake. "It's very nice to meet you, Katie. Welcome to our home." She chuckled, then added, "That was quite a greeting you received."

Katie smiled. She immediately liked this woman.

Mrs. Cassidy held Katie's hand for a moment longer and

seemed to be studying her. Then she turned to her husband and said, "Matthew, Katie could certainly pass for our daughter. She has your large hazel eyes and auburn hair."

Katie shot a triumphant look at Zack. He screwed his mouth up on one side and rolled his eyes.

Mrs. Cassidy leaned over the child in the wheelchair and said, "Katie, I want you to meet Anna, our seven-year-old angel. Anna is the one who picked out Tango at the horse sale."

Katie turned toward the frail girl and thought she looked like a delicate china sculpture. Anna's blue eyes met Katie's, and the sweetest, most innocent smile spread across Anna's face. "It's nice to meet you, Katie," she said. "I've *really* been looking forward to you coming."

Katie wasn't sure if she should shake the fragile girl's hand or not. Anna looked as though she might break if someone touched her, so Katie simply gave a self-conscious wave of her hand and said, "Hi, Anna."

Mrs. Cassidy looked lovingly at her daughter, then back over to Katie. "Anna's been talking all day about you coming here. She's so excited about having a big sister."

Katie nodded slightly, hoping the confusion and amazement over all these strange events didn't show in her face.

Mrs. Cassidy didn't seem to notice. Instead, she exclaimed, "Oh! In all the excitement I forgot—I've made chocolate chip cookies!" She turned and hurried away, returning with a plate of freshly baked temptations.

Zack yelled, "Oh boy, my favorite!" and made a dive for the plate.

Mrs. Cassidy quickly held the platter up out of his reach. "Zack, shouldn't we be polite and offer them to our guest first?" She was smiling, but Katie saw the unspoken message in her eyes as she focused on her son. Katie knew that look well.

"Oh yeah," he murmured, lowering his arm and stepping back slightly.

Mrs. Cassidy set the plate on the coffee table and motioned for Katie to have a seat on the brown leather couch. After Katie picked up a cookie, Zack's arm immediately shot out and grabbed one too. Stuffing half of it into his mouth, he mumbled around the bite, "Mom's a great cook."

As the warm chocolate melted into her mouth, Katie didn't need convincing.

Zack reached for another cookie, then turned toward Katie and said, "Mom's not just a great cook, but she can also rope anything that moves. Once she was trying to get Dad's attention outside, so as a joke she roped him and pinned his arms."

"Zack!" his father said quickly, shooting a stern look at the boy. But Katie thought Mr. Cassidy looked like he wanted to smile. She giggled a little. Even though her own mother was lots of fun, she couldn't imagine her mom ever being able to handle a rope. Mrs. Cassidy sounded like a special lady.

Mrs. Cassidy blushed as she glanced toward Zack. "Well, that's not the normal introduction I receive," she said, arching her eyebrows and smiling.

They all laughed, and Katie glanced from one to the other sitting around this warm living room. She was struck by the love and happiness she felt here.

Mrs. Cassidy broke into her thoughts. "Katie, you'd probably like to see your room and get settled in before dinner." She motioned for the girl to follow her.

"Yes, ma'am," Katie answered as she rose to follow Mrs. Cassidy through the living room and down a hallway.

After they passed a messy room on the left that had to be Zack's, Mrs. Cassidy swung open the next door, revealing a light-filled room with horse-print curtains at the window and a large, inviting bed. As Katie looked around in delight, Mrs. Cassidy walked to a closet door at the far side of the room. "I hope you don't mind," she said, opening the door, "but I went ahead and hung up your clothes. You know, once a mom, always a mom."

Katie stared in disbelief. Some of her favorite shirts hung in this guestroom closet! *How did those get here?* Realizing her mouth had dropped open, she quickly snapped it shut, then turned to Mrs. Cassidy and tried to speak calmly. "Thank you so much. You didn't have to do that—but thanks! My mom never hangs my clothes up for me. At least not any more."

"Well, I'll follow your mother's example and let you do it from now on, okay?" Mrs. Cassidy replied with another smile.

"Okay," Katie answered, still staring at her clothes.

From the corner of her eye, she saw Mrs. Cassidy glance down at Katie's dusty shorts. "You can change before dinner if you want," Mrs. Cassidy said. Katie knew that motherly voice. It *really* meant, "I'd like you to change clothes before you come to dinner."

Katie nodded. "Okay. I'll be out soon."

As Mrs. Cassidy left, gently closing the door behind her, Katie took a deep breath and sat down on the edge of the bed to try and sort through everything that had happened. *I'm living on the ranch that was in my book, and I have my own horse. But how on earth did I get here? And do I get to stay? Of course I wouldn't know how to get home even if I wanted to—which I don't, because I finally have a horse!* Confusion tumbled through Katie's mind like clothes in a dryer as she replayed everything over and over.

Hearing the clatter of dishes down the hall, Katie thought, *I really like this family—except for that pest Zack. But…Anna thinks I'll be like her big sister.* A slight frown creased her forehead. *I've never had to share my things with a sister before…and that's sure been okay with me.*

A loud bang on the door startled her. "Hey, hurry up!" called Zack. "I'm starving!"

"I'm coming!" Katie yelled back, somewhat annoyed at being interrupted. *Well, I'll just have to think about all this later.* She jumped off the bed and quickly changed in to a pair of jeans.

After washing her hands in the bathroom across the hall, Katie found the Cassidys already seated in the dining room. Mrs. Cassidy pointed to a chair beside Anna at the large oak table, and Katie sat down. The enticing aromas suddenly made her realize how incredibly hungry she was, and she immediately reached for the bowl of steaming mashed potatoes in front of her. As she did, Mr. Cassidy said, "Anna, would you like to thank the Lord for our food and for our new family member?"

Katie's arm froze in midair. *Thank the Lord?* Her family had never paused before digging in to the food on the table. *What am I supposed to do?*

Glancing around, Katie saw everyone lower their head and close their eyes. She quickly followed along—except she kept one eye open just a crack to make sure she didn't do something dumb.

"Dear Lord," began Anna's sweet voice, "thank You for bringing Katie to us. She already seems like my sister. And thank You for my wonderful family. And thank You for Mama's great food. Amen."

"Amen," the others chimed in quietly. Through Katie's half-open eye she saw everyone look up, so she quickly did the same. *Now* she could dive into the mashed potatoes.

Dinner with the Cassidy family was different from anything she had ever experienced. They were kind and polite to one another—even Zack, *the little faker.* They spoke about God a lot, and about His involvement in their lives. She'd never heard anyone talk like that before, and it made her curious.

Katie was deep into the fried chicken when she heard Mrs. Cassidy say, "So tell us about your family, Katie."

Jerking her head up, Katie stiffened for a moment. Her mind raced to think of any reason why she shouldn't tell the Cassidys about her life, but she couldn't come up with anything, so she plunged in. "Well, there's Mom and Dad, and I have two older brothers, Mark and Dave." She made a slight face when she mentioned her brothers' names, which made the others laugh.

"How old are they?" Zack asked.

"My parents?"

"No, goofball—your brothers!" Zack said.

Katie giggled as she thought about how upset her mom would have been if Katie had announced her mother's age. "Mark's fourteen and Dave is sixteen," she said. "They're okay, and Mark's pretty fun…but they like to play computer games, and they lock me out of their room."

Mrs. Cassidy said, "That must be hard sometimes." She sounded sympathetic.

Katie thought for a second, then said, "Well, I read about horses a lot, and write my own stories, so I guess it's helped me develop a pretty good imagination." Then she glanced around quickly at everyone. She hoped they didn't realize she only *read* about horses rather than actually riding them.

No one seemed to be reacting, so Katie breathed a sigh of relief and continued. "My dad works really hard at running a plant where they make shirts and pants and stuff. And Mom's great. She makes me laugh. She nicknamed me Katie. My real name is Katherine, but Mom said that when I was born I right away had a sort of impish grin. So then and there she said I definitely looked more like a Katie, and that name stuck."

Mrs. Cassidy smiled. "I definitely agree with your mother. And I know Zack and Anna will have lots of fun with you."

Katie saw Zack out of the corner of her eye. He looked uncomfortable. She could tell he wasn't quite sure how to respond to the idea of having fun with a *girl*, and he began filling his mouth with food and staring at his plate.

Mr. Cassidy must have noticed, because he changed the subject slightly. "Anna sure is eager to watch you ride," he said.

Katie's heart instantly jumped into her throat. *They're going to watch me ride? I've only ridden twice in my life on some ol' nag at summer camp!* Adrenaline surged through her body like water from a fire hose. *And why would Anna want to see me ride anyway?* Katie's thoughts were frantic as she glanced at the girl, then realized everyone was looking at her. *Maybe they'll give me time to ride around on my own first,* she thought, forcing a smile.

Zack piped up with, "Hey, why don't we have Katie show Anna how to ride Tango right after dinner? It'll still be light for a while."

Katie's head whipped toward Zack. *How could he know?* Panic flooded through her, and she suddenly wanted to run— *but how do I get out of a book?* she thought. Instead, Katie just sat there, trembling inside and waiting to see what would happen next.

"Well," Mr. Cassidy said, looking from Katie to Anna, "what do you think, Anna? Do you want to see Tango in action as soon as we're done?"

Anna's entire face lit up, and her eyes gave her answer. Yet she seemed to pick her words carefully as she said, "I'd love to see Katie ride Tango…but only if she wants to right now."

Katie tried to smile back at Anna as she thought, *I **don't** want to ride right now!* She looked quickly around the table, then back at Anna. *But how can I refuse this little girl?* Katie cleared her throat and said in a voice that sounded a bit strained,

"I'd—I would be happy to ride Tango."

For Katie, the next few minutes passed like a blur as she merely picked at the rest of her food. When Zack began clearing the dishes and Mr. Cassidy left to saddle the horse, Katie trudged into her room to get the shiny red cowboy boots she had spied in the closet. As she pulled them on, she thought, *Maybe I could act like I'm sick, or something.*

"Katie! Let's go," Mrs. Cassidy called.

Katie reluctantly appeared as Mrs. Cassidy began wheeling Anna toward the side door. Katie didn't think it was possible, but her heart sank even further when she noticed Anna excitedly bouncing up and down in her chair.

As they headed down the dirt road toward an exercise ring in front of the barn, Mrs. Cassidy looked over at Katie and said, "Anna's a real trooper. She was born with a spinal cord defect, which has weakened her legs. But she does great at therapy every week, and she's looking forward to starting horseback therapy sometime soon…aren't you, sweetheart?" she said, looking down at her daughter.

"I can't wait!" Anna said, her eyes sparkling.

Katie looked puzzled. "Horseback therapy?"

Mrs. Cassidy nodded. "It's something new we've just learned about. The therapist says that riding a horse will strengthen Anna's core muscles and help her balance. Since we don't live close enough to a big city with a therapeutic riding center, and we already do home schooling, it seemed like a logical step to try the horseback therapy on our own as well. That's why Anna's so eager to watch you ride Tango."

Nodding in response, Katie thought to herself, *I guess Anna wants to learn about riding by watching me. But why can't she just watch Zack or Mr. Cassidy ride?*

Before Katie could ask, however, Anna looked up at her mother and said in a quiet voice, "I love it out here, Mama. The smells, the colors...and best of all, the horses."

Mrs. Cassidy reached down and took Anna's small hand. The girl met her mother's eyes as Mrs. Cassidy said, "Honey, I know it's hard sometimes to watch Zack go out and ride with your father. But you know we're every bit as proud of you. Your sweet spirit is what makes you so special."

Katie heard Mrs. Cassidy's voice catch, and she saw her look away so Anna wouldn't see the tears forming in her eyes.

But Katie instantly forgot about all of that when she saw Mr. Cassidy lead Tango toward the corral and motion for her to follow. Her heart began pounding loudly again, and Katie moved slowly, her feet dragging, into the sandy arena. As Zack closed the gate behind her, she thought, *This must be how the gladiators felt when they walked into an arena full of lions.*

Katie's and Zack's eyes met, and the boy's face broke into a grin that looked as if he somehow knew this was going to be a perfect opportunity to get her back. Katie made a face at him, then turned away. Out of the corner of her eye she saw Anna just outside the fence, her pale blue eyes watching every move through the rails. Mrs. Cassidy stood beside her, gently smoothing the girl's blonde hair.

"Okay, Katie," Mr. Cassidy said, turning toward her. "Tango's all ready to go. Hop up and show us how it's done."

Hop up? Show you how it's done? Panic flowed through Katie from head to toe as she stepped toward the muscular horse. *What on earth do I do now?*

Chapter 3

Katie felt like ice was running through her veins as she placed her left foot slowly into the stirrup. Mr. Cassidy was holding Tango's reins. "Anna's picked a great looking horse," he told her. Then he looked directly at Katie and added, "It's really wonderful for us that you've got the time to come here and calm him down, Katie. Since he's been a cutting horse, he's got some pretty powerful hindquarters."

Katie bit her lip as she reached up to grab the saddlehorn. *What does he mean by "powerful hindquarters"?* she thought, her panic increasing even more. *Tango sounds fast and dangerous!*

She took a deep breath and with a slight bounce off the ground, she swung her right leg over and settled into the saddle. Swallowing hard, she took the reins from Mr. Cassidy. Her hands felt slippery with sweat. *Well, here goes nothing.*

20

But something odd was happening. *None of this feels strange!* The saddle seemed comfortable and familiar. And when she turned Tango toward the center of the ring, Katie suddenly felt like she'd done this a thousand times before.

Clucking softly to the horse, Katie moved him into an easy trot. *It feels like I was born on a horse!* she marveled as she sat straight in the saddle and moved in perfect harmony with the animal. *How is this happening?*

Katie guided Tango along the rails of the ring. As they swung past the onlookers, she saw Mrs. Cassidy catch her husband's eye and heard her say to him, "She looks good. Rides like a pro."

"She does indeed," Mr. Cassidy said, nodding approval as he climbed over the fence and joined his family.

Katie continued to move Tango around the ring, astounded at the way she instinctively knew how to shift her weight forward ever so slightly, urging Tango into the next gait. As he moved into a slow rhythmic lope, Katie swayed gently in the saddle. Communicating through small movements of her hands and legs, she felt as though her body had merged with this horse. It all seemed unbelievably natural!

Next, Katie switched Tango into a figure-eight pattern, executing perfect "flying lead changes" as she guided the horse into changing his leading leg, depending on whether they turned right or left. Tango's sturdy body rippled with muscles, and his reddish-brown tail streamed back like a flag waving gloriously in the wind as he loped around the ring.

Every time Katie rode past the group of onlookers, she

saw Anna leaning forward in her wheelchair, absorbing every move the pair made. Sometimes the young girl would clap her hands with joy.

After circling the ring a few more times, she heard Mr. Cassidy call, "Okay, Katie, you and Tango are a great team. Let's call it an evening."

Katie could still hardly believe this was happening. She had no idea why she could suddenly ride so well, knowing every move to make, every leg pressure, every hand motion. But it all felt completely natural—as if she had somehow been given this special ability when she landed on the ranch. *That must be it!* she thought. *It's some sort of miracle.*

Katie called out a soft, "Whoa," and shifted her weight back in the saddle. Tango tucked his hind legs under him, coming to a perfect stop. Out of the corner of her eye, Katie could see Zack shaking his head in wonder. A faint smile crossed her lips. She didn't know how all this was happening, but to get Zack's admiration was a sweet victory.

Dismounting, Katie patted Tango's neck and shook her head slightly. *I'm riding this incredible horse that's now mine, and I'm living on a real-live ranch. This is way too good to be true!* She stroked Tango's nose and said quietly, "Life just doesn't get any better than this, fella."

Tango flicked an ear toward her and nickered softly.

Katie led the horse over to the fence and smiled at Anna. "So, what do you think?" she asked, still basking in excitement over her new-found riding ability.

"That was great!" Anna said, clapping her hands. "You

and Tango looked perfect together." Anna focused her blue eyes on Katie and added, "Thanks so much for coming here, Katie. I can't wait till I get to ride him."

Katie's eyebrows drew together. *Anna ride Tango?* But she didn't have time to think about it further as Mr. Cassidy added, "Good job, Katie."

"Thanks," she said, dropping her head as she tried to hide another big smile.

Still looking down, Katie heard Mrs. Cassidy say, "She makes it look so easy, huh, Zack?"

Katie jerked her head up. She couldn't *wait* to hear what he'd say to that.

Zack shuffled his boots in the dirt and stared at the ground. "Well…" he said.

This must be killing him! Katie thought, grinning.

"Uh…she's okay," he finally said, barely loud enough for anyone to hear. But when he looked up and met her eyes, Katie got a real surprise. He actually looked at her as if he meant the compliment.

Before Katie could respond, Mr. Cassidy turned toward his daughter. "How do you think Tango looked, Anna?"

The girl met her father's gaze. "He's the most perfect horse I've ever seen, Daddy," she said softly. Big drops welled up in her eyes as she whispered, "Thanks so much." A few tears spilled onto the plaid blanket lying across her thin legs.

Mr. Cassidy bent down and hugged his frail daughter. "You're welcome, honey," he said. "We're looking forward to the day you can ride."

Katie saw Mrs. Cassidy look away quickly, her eyes filling up with tears too.

Mr. Cassidy stood and motioned toward Zack. "Why don't you and Katie go brush and feed Tango while I take care of a few things?"

"Okay," Katie and Zack said in unison, then they looked at each other and chuckled a little.

"We'll see you all back at the house," Mrs. Cassidy called as she began wheeling Anna away.

When Katie and Zack reached the barn, he seemed deep in thought and unusually quiet. As he handed Katie a horse brush he finally blurted out, "How'd you learn to ride like that?"

Katie couldn't think what to say. *How on earth can I answer that?* She finally shrugged and muttered, "I dunno."

Zack looked down for a second, then sharply raised his head and said, "Well...I'll bet you can't rope!"

The way things were happening in this place, Katie didn't know if she could rope or not. But how could she explain that to Zack? She decided instead to focus on the joy of having her own horse and avoid an argument. "Tango is awesome," she said. "He's so easy to ride. Anna must have an eye for horses, because she sure picked a winner."

Zack didn't respond right away, but finally said softly, "I'd give anything for Anna to ride—and especially to get well."

The sudden tenderness in Zack's voice caught Katie completely by surprise. He *could* be nice! Maybe there was hope.

After giving Tango's dark chestnut coat a good brushing, Katie led him to his stall. For the first time since arriving in this new and exciting world, she was able to truly enjoy the moment. She looked into Tango's big eyes, then threw her arms around his neck. "You *are* wonderful," she said quietly to the horse. "I've only known you a few hours, but I already love you, Tango. We're going to have so much fun together!" She buried her face in his long mane.

Tango turned his head and dropped it against her, as if returning her hug. It seemed to Katie that he sensed their special bond.

"Mushy girl," she heard Zack mumble disgustedly from outside the stall door.

Katie made a face at him, then whispered in Tango's ear, "He's just jealous because I have such an amazing horse."

After Katie and Zack filled Tango's feed bin and water bucket, they slid his stall door shut and headed toward the house. Katie didn't say anything, taking in all the wonders of this day. Zack for once seemed willing to let her remain at peace.

When they entered the living room, Mr. Cassidy looked up from some papers he was working on and said, "Katie, how about Zack and I showing you around the ranch tomorrow? We've got 400 of the best acres God ever created. We can't see it all in one day, but I'd like to show you some nice places where you can ride."

Zack jumped in. "Yeah, this is my favorite time of year. The mountain snow is mostly melted, the creek is running really high, and everything's green."

"Sounds great!" Katie said.

Bedtime came much too soon, and Katie was still so

excited she thought she'd never be able to fall asleep. But almost immediately after turning out her light, she began dreaming about Tango and the magical ranch.

It seemed like just a few minutes later a knock rattled her bedroom door. "Rise and shine!" called Mrs. Cassidy. Katie rolled over with a moan and looked at the clock on the nightstand. *Five o'clock! Who gets up at five o'clock?* she wondered in disbelief. But this was a ranch, and she had read countless stories about how ranch life begins early. Besides, today she would get to explore this enchanting place!

When Katie reached the kitchen, Mrs. Cassidy told her they did chores before breakfast, and that she could help gather the eggs.

"Me?" Katie said. She didn't have a clue how to get an egg away from a chicken.

"Zack will show you the ropes," Mrs. Cassidy said, nodding toward her son who had just appeared from the hallway, rubbing his eyes.

Zack gave his mom a desperate sort of look, then turned toward the door and waved his arm helplessly. "Come on," he said without looking at Katie.

After Katie learned how to scoop eggs out from under the docile hens, she and Zack met up with Mr. Cassidy and went down to the barn to feed and water the horses. There, Mr. Cassidy introduced her to Diego. "He's our ranch hand," Mr. Cassidy said, "and he came from Mexico with his family some years ago."

Diego held out his wide hand, and Katie shook it, feeling

26

his stubby, calloused fingers against hers. Mr. Cassidy said, "Diego is the one who *really* holds this ranch together."

Diego smiled a toothy grin as he released Katie's hand and said in a thick Spanish accent, "No, no señor. I just do my work as unto the Lord, like it says in the Good Book."

Mr. Cassidy smiled. "Well, you're our number-one ranch hand."

"I'm your *only* ranch hand, señor," Diego said, breaking into a hearty laugh that shook his entire stocky frame.

Katie knew right away she was going to like this jovial man.

Once the early morning chores were finished, Katie helped Mrs. Cassidy mix the batter for some melt-in-your-mouth pancakes, soon to be covered with maple syrup and butter. Katie also met Toby, their chocolate-brown hunting dog, who for some reason hung out close to her side.

"Oh, don't mind him," Mrs. Cassidy said as the dog's eyes followed Katie's every move. "He helps me keep the kitchen floor clean, I'm afraid."

Katie laughed when Toby hurried over to lick up a drop of batter from the floor by the stove.

As soon as they all finished breakfast, Katie raced toward the barn to saddle Tango for their trail ride. Zack and Mr. Cassidy were finishing up their chores someplace, so she had the freedom to carry on a real conversation with her horse.

"You're the best horse in the world," she said, looking intently into his dark brown eyes. "I don't know how I got here, but I wouldn't trade this for *anything*! I don't want to go home.

How could I ever give you up?" She threw her arms around his neck. "You're what I've wanted my whole life!" She felt like her heart might burst with love and excitement.

Suddenly Katie sensed the presence of someone else in the barn. At first, she thought Mr. Cassidy and Zack had returned. But when she turned to look, all she could see was the silhouette of a large man in the barn doorway. He was wearing a straw Panama hat, and she could tell he was quite tall and maybe around fifty years old. *Really old,* she thought. He also looked powerful because of his size. Not overweight—just strong. And maybe a bit scary.

As Katie stared at the figure, something seemed vaguely familiar about him, but she couldn't figure out why. It unnerved her a little that he didn't say a word, but just stood there looking at her. And even though she couldn't see his eyes against the bright sunlight behind him, she had a weird feeling that he was looking right through her—maybe even reading her mind.

Katie decided to break the ominous silence. "Hello," she said cautiously, her voice betraying her uneasiness.

The stranger took a slow step forward, and Katie could now see his eyes looking into hers. He no longer seemed as frightening, but she somehow knew this was no ordinary man.

Suddenly he spoke words in a low, deep voice. "Katie Carlson, I know who you are, I know where you came from, and I know why you are here."

CHAPTER 4

Of course Katie couldn't know that ninety miles away from the Cassidy Ranch, other events had been unfolding the night before that eventually would affect her life as well.

A young man sat on his dirty mattress inside a small bunkhouse, rubbing the bottom of his right foot. He noticed several of his toes sticking out through the threadbare sock. Both feet throbbed from standing all day branding cattle.

"Got some achin' tootsies there, Roberto?" Gunny said with a grin, revealing several missing teeth.

A scowl creased Roberto's face as he looked up at the ranch foreman. "Yeah. That stinkin' Parker wouldn't let me take a break all day," he said, continuing to massage his sore foot. "You heard him. Every time I tried to rest, he'd start screamin' at me to get back to work." Roberto dropped his eyes and mumbled, "Should have branded *him* with the hot iron."

Gunny shook his head. In his heavy western drawl, he said, "Ya shouldn'ta spouted off to him the other day, kid. Jeremiah Parker, well, he's the boss. And he don't forgive none too easily."

"He insulted my heritage!" Roberto shot back. "I'm proud of being Mexican. We're some of the hardest working people in this country!"

Gunny smiled slightly. "Well, even if that's true," he said, "ya still better learn to keep your mouth shut." A twinkle came into his gray eyes as he added, "That purty face of yours ain't gonna git ya no pats on the back here."

Roberto responded by flinging a pillow at the foreman. He was tired of the guys constantly taunting him about looking like some sort of cowboy model, with a "handsome, rugged face and strong, broad shoulders." To Roberto, none of that mattered in the midst of this depressing world. "I'm not looking for pats on the back," he said. "But I *would* like to be treated like a human being."

Gunny had easily dodged the pillow and turned to face the young man again. Slowly, he said, "Kid, if ya hate it here so much, why ain't ya gone back home?"

Roberto looked down at his grimy mattress. *Why don't I go home?* he asked himself. *I'm working like a dog for a boss who's meaner than a snake, and I don't even get paid that well. What am I doing?* Roberto thought for a minute, then squared his shoulders and looked up defiantly at Gunny. Two other ranch hands had come into the room, and they turned with interest to hear his reply. "Go home?" Roberto said, hoping he sounded tough. "My ol' man wouldn't have me back."

Walt, the oldest of the four now in the conversation, took a step toward Roberto. "I dunno, kid," he said. "I've met Diego, and he's one of the nicest guys around. Besides, from what I hear, you had it pretty great at the Cassidy place." Walt nodded his large head, making his thinning gray hair flop up and down. "Yup…they're good people," he added quietly.

Roberto was looking into Walt's brown eyes. He marveled at how the older cowboy had been able to maintain a kind and gentle heart through all his years of grueling ranch work. *Particularly working for Parker.*

Walt's words made Roberto remember that day, shortly after he'd turned seventeen, when he had run away from home. He'd never called his parents, so they had no idea where he was living—or even *if* he was living. For a month or so he'd drifted around, hitchhiking and stealing and getting into bar fights, until the night Walt had picked him up off some floor and brought him here to Jeremiah Parker's ranch.

At the thought of having lived here for over two years, Roberto automatically clenched his teeth. *I'm working harder than I thought was humanly possible, I've been repeatedly lied to and cheated by Parker, and for all this rotten backbreaking effort, I still don't have a dime to show for it,* he thought bitterly. Roberto wasn't so sure Walt had done him a favor.

Buster, the fourth ranch hand in the dingy room, had arrived only a week ago. He interrupted Roberto's thoughts with a question. "Why *did* you leave home, Roberto? From what

Walt says, you had it a lot better at that Cassidy place than you do here."

Roberto pushed thick black hair away from his eyes as he turned to look at Buster. The bitterness he felt slowly melted into utter defeat as he said, "I don't know. Just a stupid kid, I guess. I was seventeen and tired of my parents' rules an' all. I thought I knew a whole lot more than they did, and I wanted to prove it." Roberto paused for a second, then added, "I guess 'cause I was the first one of my family born here in the States, I wanted to prove I could do better than my ol' man."

Gunny broke into a hoarse laugh. "And here you are just like him, workin' as a ranch hand—but in conditions far *worse* than your pa's!" He slapped the small nightstand near Roberto's bed, making the dim lamp jump. "That's purty funny, all right!"

Roberto didn't find anything humorous about it. He was maybe coming to understand all the effort and patience his mom and dad had made to raise him with good morals, a decent education, and a faith in God. But he'd left it all behind—and realized he was paying dearly for that choice.

Gunny's laughter had died away, and Roberto tried to push thoughts of his home and family far from his mind, like he tried to do every day. Most of the time it wasn't too hard. Mr. Parker worked him so relentlessly that Roberto either didn't have time to think about what he had lost, or he was just plain too exhausted.

A tiny wisp of dust rose as Roberto fell back on his mattress and let out a dejected sigh. More to himself than to the guys he muttered, "Mom and Dad worked awfully hard to give me the things they didn't have growing up. I guess I took it all for granted, because I just wanted to be free. I had no idea that men like Jeremiah Parker even existed."

"Yeah," Gunny said, his narrow, leathery face growing serious. "He'll promise you one thing, then always do somethin' else, that's for sure."

Roberto snorted. "I can't tell you how many times that buzzard has promised me a raise, only to come back and tell me I wouldn't get it because I'm a lousy worker. Or he'll accuse me of breaking some piece of equipment. Or best of all, he'll tell me I can't be trusted." Roberto gave a cynical laugh as he sat upright again. "There's a joke—the biggest liar on earth telling me *I* can't be trusted!"

Walt nodded sympathetically. "Yup, all you'll get from Parker are lies. Not a drop of integrity in him. He's a man who only knows God as a swear word."

Roberto thought about how he would love to leave Parker's ranch—but go where? *I don't know any other ranch outfits close by that need help, and I don't have any money for a bus ticket. Besides, where would I take a bus to anyway?*

As Buster turned the lights out, Roberto flopped back on his bunk again. Sleep, however, wouldn't come quickly this night. He couldn't keep his mind from recalling the feel of his mother's loving arms around him, the joy of laughing with his father and with the Cassidys, and the privilege of being treated with respect and dignity. *But how can I return home now?* He cringed as he remembered stealing his father's savings, and how quickly he'd spent it all. *And I'm sure I've broken my mom's heart.*

How could I ever go back? Roberto groaned softly. *I feel like a bear caught in a trap that I made myself. And now I don't know how to get out of it.*

The next morning, work began even earlier than usual at the Parker ranch. As the shrill bell rang through the bunkhouse, Roberto rolled his weary body from the hard bed. Nausea rose inside him just looking at his boots at the foot of the bunk, knowing he had to face another day of work on this ranch. Today Mr. Parker wanted all the cattle from the back country herded into the holding pens by the barn, because tomorrow they would transport some of those steers to a local rodeo to be used in their roping contest.

As Roberto fished under his bed for a pair of socks with fewer holes, he thought about the enormity of Parker's ranch. It certainly dwarfed the Cassidy place. Over 1,000 head of cattle ranged these 20,000 acres. And to reach the cattle in the back country, they would have to trailer the horses in as far as the road allowed, then ride in the rest of the way and herd the skittish critters out. *Another backbreaking day on this lousy ranch.*

Roberto got dressed and plopped down at the small wooden table in the corner of the bunkhouse. Today was Walt's turn to cook breakfast—and everyone dreaded those mornings. Roberto stabbed his fork into a yellowish glob on his plate and lifted it hesitantly to his mouth. He began to chew and screwed his face up as he tried to swallow, then pushed the plate away. "Eww! These eggs taste like sawdust!"

Walt grinned. "Maybe they are. Maybe we ran out of eggs last night."

Roberto made a face at him and said, "Walt, how on earth can you ruin *eggs*?"

"It's my mother's recipe," Walt replied with another grin.

"Just give me some coffee," Roberto mumbled, holding his stained mug up. He knew at least tomorrow he'd have a good breakfast since it was his turn to cook. Thankfully, his sweet mom had taken the pains to teach him how to make decent meals.

After quickly downing a cup of strong, bitter coffee, Roberto threw on his jacket and stepped from the bunkhouse into the chilly morning air. The sun was still half an hour from rising, and the cold bit into his bones.

At the barn, Gunny and Buster had already led their horses from the stalls and loaded them into the horse trailer. Walt joined Roberto in the barn as they strapped halters on their horses and led them toward the trailer. Puffs of steam rose from the horses' nostrils as they snorted with anticipation.

Roberto returned to the barn and gathered the remaining saddles, blankets, and bridles they would need, then slid into the truck's front seat across from Gunny. The foreman eased the long rig out of the yard, and they headed down a wide gravel track.

As the truck and trailer moved onto a rutted dirt path, the four men rode silently, each sipping strong coffee from metal cups. Gunny carefully maneuvered the rig up and down hills and around blind corners, working their way deeper and deeper into the ranch land. Periodically the horses' hooves would bang and pound inside the metal trailer as they shifted their weight or regained their footing around corners. "Them horses sound restless back there," Gunny said, more to himself than to anyone.

Roberto glanced over at the lean, thirty-eight-year-old man. He knew Gunny had worked here for ten years and received far more respect and pay than any other employee, because Mr. Parker needed him. *He deserves it,* Roberto thought with a slight shrug. *Anyone that can put up with Parker for ten years deserves every penny!*

One of the men sitting behind Roberto sneezed. Roberto turned around to see Buster, only a few years older than himself, wiping his nose across his sleeve. "Need a handkerchief?" Roberto asked.

Buster looked up. "Nope. I'm fine," he said as he took a final wipe half way up his arm.

Roberto saw Walt shake his head in disgust, and their eyes met. Roberto shrugged again and turned back to face forward. He did admire Walt. The man had endured six years on Parker's ranch after the place he'd been working shut down. Like the other three cowboys in the truck, Walt had no wife or children, so he was free to drift and wander. Roberto knew that Walt was almost fifty years old, with little ambition to fight his way into a different career. Walt had told him once that even though Parker was a man of minimal character, ranch hand jobs were few and far between in this modern computer age, so he was just going to hang on.

Roberto gazed absently out the front window at the various trails crisscrossing the enormous property. But when Buster sneezed again, Roberto started thinking about the day, one week ago, when the young man had wandered on to this ranch looking for a job. His timing had been perfect, since another man had quit in disgust the night before. Gunny had given Buster a quick interview, watched him ride a horse, and hired him on the spot. More than once, Roberto had secretly urged the new ranch hand to "light outta here as fast as you can!" Just yesterday Buster had confessed that he was beginning to think Roberto might be right.

The truck lurched, and Roberto saw that their path ahead disappeared into a dense grove of trees. Gunny moved the gear shift into park and said, "Looks like this here's 'bout as far as we're gonna git."

"How far to the back pasture?" Buster asked.

"'Bout a twenty-minute ride," Gunny said as he climbed out the door.

Roberto stepped out of the truck and noticed that the sun had finally broken over the horizon. Its warming rays around him felt like a blanket fresh from the clothes dryer. *Another reminder of Mom.* He stretched, then studied the trails before them. He knew that all the deep valleys, steep hills, and muddy creek beds kept the truck from reaching much of these 20,000 acres. Many areas had to be covered on horseback or foot—and those were the places where the cattle especially loved to hide.

Buster lowered the trailer door and helped back the horses down. As each man began saddling his mount, Walt handed out packs filled with food and water for the long day ahead. Roberto took the pack, then looked at Walt in alarm. "You didn't make the lunch, did you?"

"Worried?" Walt laughed as he placed a hand on Roberto's shoulder. "It's okay—Antonia made the meal."

"Whew!" Roberto sighed. He loved the ranch cook's food. Of course *any* food was better than Walt's.

"Let's move out!" Gunny called as they mounted and turned their horses toward the back pasture.

Roberto couldn't see the pasture from here, but he had been back there once before and remembered its beauty. However, it was a challenge to reach. On top of that, once they found the hundred head of cattle back there, herding them out wouldn't be easy. Since the animals had been isolated for a while, they would want to run from everything—which made them perfect for a rodeo roping contest.

Silently the four men started weaving their way through thick groves of oak and pine trees. Little by little the trail narrowed and began winding downward until they finally emerged from the heavy growth into the mouth of a long, narrow gorge. Roberto scanned the walls of the canyon that rose sharply on each side, then looked at the small creek trickling down the middle. He knew the only way out was either forward along the stream or back the way they'd just come.

As they rode into the valley, Roberto snapped his jacket shut. He remembered it was always colder in here, since the sun's rays could only reach over these walls for a few hours each day. In the stillness of the morning air, a hawk's cry from overhead echoed off the canyon sides.

Roberto gazed up at the almost-vertical sides of the gorge,

then turned to Walt and said softly, "I like it in here. It's so quiet and isolated."

"And cold and dark," Walt said, pulling his jacket a bit closer around his thick chest and waist. He glanced at the steep walls that surrounded them and added quickly, "I'd hate to get caught in here."

Roberto didn't respond. He just liked the peacefulness of this place. *Any* place felt peaceful when he was far away from Jeremiah Parker.

In a short time the men reached the far end of the confined gorge, and the entire landscape changed dramatically. Roberto quickly scanned the area, noticing how the canyon walls seemed to almost evaporate into broad rolling fields. Large old Ponderosa pines and Bur oaks dotted the land, some looking as if they'd stood guard here for hundreds of years. The pasture rose and fell in gentle waves of thick green grass.

Roberto heard Buster whistle in admiration and say softly, "Will ya look at that!"

Gunny turned in his saddle. "Yeah, Buster, it's purty all right. Some a' them trees must be older'n this country. 'Course that means they can be mighty brittle, too. Them big ol' branches can suddenly break off with a powerful crack an' spook the cows."

Buster smiled. "Just enjoy the view, Gunny. Don't look for the problems."

"I'm paid to look for problems," Gunny answered gruffly.

About twenty Black Angus raised their heads at the sound of the intruders. Roberto knew the other cattle would be scattered throughout the rolling hills. As he looked over the pasture, he heard Gunny call out, "Let's git to the far end and work our way back up here."

The cowboys spent the next several hours chasing cows that weren't particularly cooperative. Roberto could have sworn that one little ornery steer was definitely enjoying a game of hide and seek. But finally the men managed to herd all the cattle together at the front of the pasture to begin the long drive back toward the ranch.

Roberto rode ahead so he could guide the cattle in the right direction once they reached the end of the canyon. The other three men rode behind the herd, funneling them through the narrow passage.

As Roberto neared the end of the gorge, he thought he heard Gunny's familiar "He-yah!" He turned around in his saddle to try and see if the last of the cattle had entered the valley. At that very moment, something sounding like a gun shot pierced the air! Roberto's startled horse bolted at the sound, and suddenly Roberto found himself face down on the ground while an enormous crash echoed throughout the steep canyon walls.

Slightly dazed from the fall, Roberto rose to his knees, lifted his head—and found himself face to face with the terrified, stampeding herd!

CHAPTER 5

Katie felt like she was frozen in place. She stared at the large man in the barn doorway and swallowed hard. It was one of those rare moments when she found herself speechless. *How does he know about me?* she thought frantically. *Is he going to tell the Cassidys, and I'll be sent back?* Questions flooded her mind as she stood there, unable to say a word.

The man took a couple of steps toward her, and Katie could finally see him clearly. The way he stood tall in a dark shirt and black pants made him look like someone prominent and important, but his gentle smile also made him seem a lot less scary.

Katie finally blurted out, "Who are you?"

The smile broadened across his wide face. "You can call me Mr. Gateman," he said. "I'm the man who sold Tango to

41

the Cassidys, and I told them this special horse came with a girl. Of course, that girl is you."

"But how did you know that? And…and you know where I came from?" she asked hesitantly.

"Yes," Mr. Gateman said nodding his head, his straw hat bobbing up and down a little. "I know about Mark and Dave and your mom and dad."

Katie was starting to feel frustrated. This man's answers were only creating *more* questions. But because she'd never been one to give up, she said, "How do you know my family?" Focusing on his dark eyes she added, "*I've* never met you."

Mr. Gateman tilted his head ever so slightly, and all of a sudden Katie gasped. Her eyes grew wide as she said, "Oh! Were you…was it…was it *you* I saw by my house when I got pulled into the book?"

Instead of answering her question, however, Mr. Gateman spread his arms and said, "Katie, think of me as your gateway to adventure and learning."

Katie's jaw dropped. "You have the power to transport me through space?"

Mr. Gateman smiled. "I work for the One with that power, Katie. I'm just here to help guide you."

"Guide me where?" she said, feeling utterly confused.

Mr. Gateman paused, becoming serious again. "Katie, you're on a ranch, just like you've always wanted—but you've been brought here for a purpose."

"What purpose?" Katie asked, her eyebrows drawing down. She thought for a second, then said, "I know. I get to ride Tango and calm him down."

The gentleman's serious expression turned into a smile again, and Katie thought he looked like he was somewhat amused. "That's only a part of the reason you are here," he said. Then he looked deeply into her eyes. "Yes, you are to calm Tango down… but ultimately it's all for Anna."

"What?" Katie's mouth dropped open. "*Anna?* But…but I thought Tango was *my* horse." She shifted her weight from one foot to the other as this nasty new information sank in. *That's why Anna has been so excited about watching me ride. Anna thinks Tango will be hers.*

Mr. Gateman took a step closer and seemed to study her face. "Katie," he said in a fatherly-sounding voice, "you have some choices to make. Only you can make them. And in the process, you will learn something very important."

Katie lowered her eyes to the barn floor. "Like what?" she muttered.

Mr. Gateman waited until she looked up again. "I can't give you all the answers right now, Katie," he said, "but I will tell you that it is up to you when Anna rides Tango. She won't ask you or push you. You'll need to offer."

Katie looked away again and began chewing on a fingernail. *I don't want to give Tango to Anna,* she griped silently. *I finally get a horse of my own, and now I'm supposed to give him up. It's not fair!*

"And there's something else," Mr. Gateman said as she continued to avoid his eyes. "But…actually, I don't think it's the right time to tell you yet."

43

How can it get any worse? Katie kept her eyes turned away for fear Mr. Gateman would recognize what she was really feeling in her heart. She kicked at some straw and sent a few pieces flying across the stall. When Mr. Gateman didn't say anything, however, she finally looked up.

The man was gone! He had vanished just as quickly as he'd appeared. Now, instead of Mr. Gateman's silhouette in the barn doorway, she saw a medium-sized boy with red hair and freckles. *Oh great!* she thought. *Just who I need to see right now.*

Katie quickly turned her back on Zack and pretended to be adjusting Tango's saddle. Trying to hide her emotions, she snapped, "What took you so long?"

"Good grief!" Zack said. "You don't have to bite my head off!"

Katie instantly felt sort of bad for taking her frustration out on Zack. "I'm sorry," she said, her voice low. She took a peek at him.

"Huh?" Zack said, surprise registering all over his face. A pink flush came into his cheeks as he said barely loud enough for her to hear, "Uh…well…uh, that's okay." He quickly began fidgeting with a halter hanging near the stall, then finally cleared his throat and said, "Ready to see the ranch?"

"Yes!" Katie said, happy to think about something other than the awful news she had just received.

Mr. Cassidy came into the barn, and he and Zack quickly saddled the horses. As they all mounted up and headed down the dirt road leading away from the house, a cheerful voice called to them from behind, "Have a good ride, amigos." They turned

pressure on his bridle. But the dilemma in her heart didn't go away as quickly as simply loosening Tango's reins.

After riding through the grove and up a gradual hill, the little group passed through another gate into a broad valley. "Seventy-five of 'em," Mr. Cassidy said proudly, nodding toward the brown cows contentedly munching on the early summer grass. Katie giggled when she saw a couple of hungry calves poke their noses under their mamas' udders to nurse.

As the riders approached, the cattle stopped chewing and turned their big round eyes toward them. Mr. Cassidy swiveled in his saddle and said to Katie, "These are mostly Jerseys. We have about twenty-five Black Angus in another field."

Katie thought their adorable faces and large eyes had a child-like innocence. "They look so sweet," she said.

Zack snickered. "Sweet. That's a girl for you, Dad. She thinks our cattle are *sweet*."

Mr. Cassidy chuckled. "Well, Katie, I guess in a way they are. They're pretty helpless and defenseless. They need us to look after them."

Katie nodded as she met the gaze of a small tan calf. Seemingly startled by her attention, it quickly scampered to its mother's opposite side, then peaked around at her with curious eyes. That made Katie giggle again.

The trio continued up and down velvety green hillsides and wound around shimmering aspens and tall pines until they reached a level pasture where the Black Angus were kept. Katie saw the jet-black cattle standing bunched together off to the left. Then she spotted a couple of cows to the right, separated from the herd. "Why are those two lying down over there?" she asked, pointing. "Are they sick?"

Mr. Cassidy narrowed his eyes, and immediately his face grew serious as he studied the two cows. When he spoke, his voice sounded strained. Over his shoulder he said, "They aren't lying down. They're dead."

CHAPTER 6

Katie felt her knees go weak as she glanced at the two motionless animals. "Dead?" she whispered.

Mr. Cassidy didn't answer. He loped Blaze over toward the two cows. Katie started to follow, but Zack put his arm out to stop her. "Katie," he said in a voice she'd never heard from him before, "this isn't going to be pretty. I'm not sure you want to look."

"What do you mean?"

Zack called out to his father who was now off his horse and examining the fallen animals. "Dad, should I bring Katie over?"

Mr. Cassidy looked up. "Well," he paused for a second, "Katie, do you want to see what a mountain lion can do to defenseless cattle? Unfortunately, it's part of life on a ranch."

A mountain lion! Katie wasn't so sure she really wanted to see this. But then again, how could she act like a scaredy cat with Zack watching her? She nodded bravely. "I want to see it."

"Okay, son, bring her over."

Katie and Zack rode their horses close to the mauled animals. Zack was right—it wasn't pretty. Katie looked away quickly.

Mr. Cassidy remounted Blaze and turned to go, indicating that she and Zack were to follow him. As they left the pasture, he turned to Katie and said, "We're grateful this doesn't happen very often, but since we live beside the Roosevelt National Forest, we have to expect occasional visits by wild animals."

Katie nodded, but was unable to say anything. The awful picture she'd just seen had made her feel sick.

Mr. Cassidy continued, "Those animals lived here before we did. And as towns and ranches eat up more and more of their land, they're forced to try and survive in much smaller areas than they used to. Cattle are an easy prey. Unfortunately, once a mountain lion has attacked a cow, he'll tend to keep coming back. It's like handing him a juicy steak."

"What can you do?" Katie asked softly.

"We're heading home to call the game warden, since our cell phones don't work out here," Mr. Cassidy said. "The warden will come out with some dogs and try to tree the cougar."

"Cougar?"

"That's another name for a mountain lion," Mr. Cassidy answered. "And if they can force the big cat up a tree, then the warden will stun it with a tranquilizer and move it to a safer place, maybe deep inside the National Forest."

The trio rode the rest of the way back in silence. When they reached the barn, Zack offered to take care of Blaze so Mr. Cassidy could go call the game warden.

"What happens now?" Katie asked as she and Zack unsaddled and brushed the horses.

"The warden will come out as quickly as possible and try to find the mountain lion," he said. "They usually come out the same day they get the call, because then there's a better chance of locating the cat. One of those steers was killed not long ago—maybe this morning or last night. The other one looked like it had gone down a couple of days ago. So the mountain lion shouldn't be too far away."

"Do they attack people?" Katie asked with a quick glance toward the barn door.

Zack grinned. "Worried?"

Katie shot him a look of annoyance. "I just wondered," she said crossly.

Zack smiled a little, then his face turned serious. "Well, not usually. Every now and then you get a mountain lion that's gone a bit loco and will attack a person. When that happens, it has to be put down, because it will keep killing."

"Put down?" Katie had never heard that term before.

Zack made a slashing motion across his throat along with gasping sounds.

Katie cringed, then rolled her eyes. *Boys! Why do they always have to be so gross?*

Mr. Cassidy appeared in the barn doorway. "Good news.

The game warden will be here in an hour. Diego and I will go back out with him and see what we can find."

Zack's green eyes lit up. "Can I come too?"

"Not this time, Zack," Mr. Cassidy said, his voice somber. "Mountain lions are nothing to fool around with. We don't know how hungry or crazy it is." Then with a slight smile he added, "I'd rather keep my right-hand man here around the house, okay?"

Zack looked down and brushed at the straw a little with his boot, but replied, "Yes, sir."

After getting the horses and tack put away, Katie joined the Cassidys for lunch. Just as they were finishing off some thick hamburgers, the game warden drove up. Mr. Cassidy hurried out to get Diego, and the two men joined the warden and his tracking dogs in the truck. As they wheeled out toward the far pasture, Katie noticed the warden's gun through the back window and guessed from what Mr. Cassidy had told her that it was loaded with tranquilizers. Mr. Cassidy and Diego also carried guns. Zack told her those guns had real bullets—just in case.

Zack went to do some chores, so Katie's only choice seemed to be spending the afternoon with Anna and Mrs. Cassidy. When Anna heard that Katie would be inside with them for a while, her blue eyes lit up. "Wanna play a game?"

"Uh…okay," Katie said, knowing she really didn't have any alternative.

Anna motioned toward her room. "Let's play with the horses."

"Go ahead," Mrs. Cassidy said with a nod. "I'll have a snack ready shortly."

Katie wheeled Anna toward the young girl's bedroom, and almost gasped when she pushed open the door. It looked so much like her own room back home! Several horse statues stood proudly on Anna's pale pink carpet, and pictures of famous racehorses hung from the walls. Katie had the feeling that the horses' eyes were following her around the room.

Anna slid to the floor, and for about an hour she and Katie pretended to be cowboys riding over vast prairies and through impossible mountain passes, braving fierce storms and ferocious wild animals. Katie couldn't help it, but she found herself drawn toward Anna's sweetness—which only increased Katie's internal dilemma.

After a while, Mrs. Cassidy called, "Snack time!" from down the hall.

"Something smells great!" Katie said as she wheeled Anna out to join her mom in the living room.

Mrs. Cassidy set a plate of fresh-from-the-oven cinnamon toast on the coffee table, and the two girls eagerly devoured the warm bread covered in butter. As they talked and laughed, Katie kept thinking there was something different about this family. She didn't know why, but their lives had a sort of—what was it?—maybe a type of joyfulness she'd never encountered before.

Just as Katie finished licking the last bit of sugary cinnamon off her fingers, she heard the sound of gravel crunching underneath a vehicle's tires. She ran outside to meet the returning hunters, and reached the truck about the same time as Zack. The game warden told them that they hadn't been able to locate the mountain lion. Then the man turned toward Mr. Cassidy and said with a wink, "I don't know, Matthew. Maybe the cougar's had his fill of prime rib and is heading somewhere else for his dessert."

"I hope it doesn't go after someone else's herd," Mr. Cassidy said as he extended his hand to the warden. "Thanks for coming out anyway."

As the man prepared to leave, he reached inside his truck and pulled out the tranquilizer gun. "Just in case you spot the cat," he said, handing it to Mr. Cassidy.

Matthew Cassidy thanked him again and said, "I'll let you know if we see anything."

As the warden drove away, Zack asked eagerly, "Did you find any tracks?"

"Yes, but they disappeared off the property," answered his father, "so we think the mountain lion may be gone. I hope so. It's a challenge to find them during the day, because they usually lay low until dusk—and then they're hard to locate."

The rest of the afternoon Katie spent goofing around with Zack. She discovered that just like her brothers, Zack *could* be fun if he wanted to be. He had evidently decided that since there was no one else to hang out with, he'd better be nice to this girl. So they actually had a great time climbing in some of the tall oak trees by the house, then playing a board game with the family after dinner.

As Katie snuggled deep into her warm bed that night, she couldn't stop smiling. *What a day! Tango is perfect! And this ranch and Mr. and Mrs. Cassidy are the best. Playing with Anna and Zack was fun too. And meeting Mr. Gateman—well, that was weird.* Her smile suddenly faded as she recalled his unwelcome words about her real purpose in being on the ranch. *Oh yeah, and he said I was supposed to learn something here, and that there was something else he couldn't tell me yet.* Katie squeezed her eyes tight. *I don't want to think about all that right now. I just want to ride Tango forever,* she thought as she dropped off to sleep.

The next morning, Mr. and Mrs. Cassidy decided it would be safe for Zack and Katie to ride their horses in an area near the house. No mountain lion tracks had ever been seen that close, and that section of the ranch was mostly open hills, which they said cougars tended to avoid, especially during daylight.

Saddling their horses in the barn, Katie looked quickly to check if Zack could see her, then she gave Tango a kiss on his velvety nose. Rising up on her toes to reach his ear she whispered, "I love you."

Tango gazed back at her with eyes that looked as if he understood.

Throwing her arms around his neck, Katie felt her heart becoming even more attached to this magnificent animal. He flicked an ear toward her as she whispered, "You know, I've never really had to share my things before—and I'm pretty sure I don't want to start now. Besides," she paused, "I'm not even sure Anna *should* ride you."

"Ready?" Zack called.

"Okay," she said, quickly peeking underneath Tango's neck to see where Zack was. Thankfully he seemed far enough away so that he couldn't have heard her conversation with her horse.

Katie and Zack rode down the dirt road and into the same field again, but this time they took the trail to the right, which kept them fairly close to the ranch house. For half an hour or so they wandered up and down hills that Katie thought looked like rolling green waves of an ocean. Occasionally a large oak offered shade under its wide leafy branches.

When they reached the top of one particularly high hill, Zack stopped and turned Bucky toward the west. Katie noticed how Zack's red hair seemed to almost glow in the daylight. He looked lost in thought as he scanned the mountains on the far horizon.

Katie turned to follow his gaze—and caught her breath in wonder! She'd been so preoccupied with the joy of riding Tango that she'd hardly looked around all morning. But there in the distance, remarkable snow-capped peaks sparkled in the sunlight, outlined sharply against the backdrop of a brilliant blue sky. Clouds hung above the jagged ridges like giant balls of cotton candy, and a hawk soared lazily around one of the distant pinnacles.

"Not bad, huh?" Zack said softly.

"It's awesome!"

Zack continued to stare at the sight before them, and spoke almost as if to himself. "God does amazing work."

"Uh huh," Katie said, not quite sure how to respond.

After a few minutes they headed back down the hill, taking a steeper path than the one they'd ridden up. This trail led through a few more trees, and the ground remained soft in the spots where sunlight seldom reached. Katie carefully followed

Zack, leaning back in her saddle because of the steep grade and giving Tango plenty of rein down the incline so he could pick his own footing.

As they neared the bottom, Zack abruptly pulled Bucky up. Katie stopped Tango right behind him and said, "What are you doing?" in a voice that *really* meant, "What dumb thing are you doing now?"

But Zack didn't respond. Instead, he held up a hand for her to be quiet. Katie immediately realized something serious was going on.

Leaning down in his saddle, Zack intently studied the ground, then moved Bucky forward a few steps deeper into the shade of a large tree. Staring hard at the dirt, he said softly, "Mountain lion tracks."

Katie quickly moved up beside him, her eyes wide with curiosity. "Really?"

"Yeah, they're all over the place," he said, motioning with his hand as he moved Bucky forward again.

Suddenly Zack sat straight up in his saddle. "We'd better get into the sunlight," he said, turning Bucky away from the tree. "It'll be safer there," he added over his shoulder.

But instead of following him, Katie dismounted and held Tango's reins while she knelt down to study the impressions in the soft soil. *Look at the size of those paws!* she thought, putting her hand over one of the large imprints.

At that moment, Tango snorted loudly from behind her and jerked the reins out of her hand. Katie looked around in time to see him bolt away and fly past Zack and Bucky at a gallop. Puzzled, she hollered after him, "Tango! What—?"

Katie saw Zack whirl around in his saddle, and a look of horror came over his face. "Katie, freeze!" he screamed.

Katie followed Zack's eyes to the hill directly above her. There crouched the mountain lion, its yellow eyes fastened… right on her!

CHAPTER 7

On his knees now, Roberto found himself staring into the eyes of a stampeding herd of cattle! In a second they would be on top of him.

Taking a flying leap to his left, Roberto was hoping to press his body against the narrow canyon wall—but he was an instant too late. In midair, he was struck by one of the frightened steers, the animal's head flipping him hard against the canyon wall.

Roberto knew he needed to grab hold of something and stay plastered against the side of the gorge if he had any chance of surviving this stampede. His hands desperately snatched for something—anything—he could hang on to. Frantically grabbing several rocks protruding from the hard-packed dirt and stones, he held himself slightly above the valley floor as the rest of the cattle rushed by.

Searing pain began radiating through Roberto's right side as he precariously hung several feet above the ground. Within seconds the pain became so intense that he was afraid he'd lose his grip, or maybe even lose consciousness—either of which would prove fatal at this moment. *Hold on!* his mind screamed. *Stay conscious! Don't black out!*

As the last of the stampede thundered by, Roberto's fingers slid from the rocks, and he dropped to the ground with a hard thud and excruciating pain. Doubling over with his arms circling his ribs, he groaned and swayed. *I can't pass out,* he kept telling himself through clenched teeth. He squeezed his eyes shut until he heard Gunny's voice over him.

"You okay?" Gunny asked, kneeling beside him.

Roberto tried to look up at the foreman. *Does it **look** like I'm okay?* he wanted to say, but all that came out was a low moan.

Walt had hurried over and lowered himself to his knees beside Gunny. Roberto saw Walt's heavy eyebrows knit together in concern as he looked at him.

Roberto managed to mumble, "What happened?"

Walt shifted to where he could look into Roberto's eyes and said, "One of those old branches broke off and scared the herd. They just about ran over each other to get through the canyon."

"They just about ran over *me*," Roberto said hoarsely.

Gunny stood and said to Walt, "We gotta git him back to the house. But we also gotta git them cattle herded back t'gether." Roberto saw the foreman wave toward the pasture beyond. "Buster can't do it by hisself," the man said.

"How on earth are we going to get him home?" Walt asked, glancing around the remote valley. "We can't get the truck in here, and now he doesn't even have a horse."

Gunny thought for a moment, then said, "He's gonna have t' git hisself home, I'm afraid."

Walt rose to face Gunny. "How?" he asked with a deep frown.

Now laying on his back at their feet, Roberto answered the question, his voice sounding strained even to himself. "I can ride. If you get me on the back of one of your horses and then to the truck, I'll drive it back to the ranch."

Gunny and Walt looked at him, then looked at each other. Walt shook his head, but Gunny turned back to Roberto and said, "Okay, kid. We'll put ya behind Walt and git ya to the truck."

Roberto held his side and started to struggle upright. Walt took his arm and helped lift him. "What part of you hurts?"

Roberto smiled weakly. "Every part."

Walt tried to return his smile, but Roberto could see the worry in his friend's eyes, so he attempted to answer the question clearly. "I'm pretty sure I've got some broken or cracked ribs," Roberto said. "Other than that, I think I'm okay. I'm just glad to still be alive."

"Amen to that!" Walt said.

Roberto stared into the man's face. That was the first time he'd ever heard Walt say anything remotely religious.

As Gunny and Walt hoisted him up on the back of Walt's

horse, Roberto had to clench his teeth so hard he thought his jaw might crack. Then Walt mounted and rode as slowly and carefully as he could out of the canyon and up the hill through the thick grove of pine and oak trees. Every one of the horse's steps felt like a knife being twisted into Roberto's side, but he tried not to groan, because he'd always heard that "cowboys don't whine." Occasionally, however, a moan escaped in spite of his efforts to stifle it.

Gunny had gone to help Buster round up the cattle, so no one else was around when Walt and Roberto finally arrived at the truck. Walt dismounted, then helped Roberto slide off. "Are you *sure* you can drive?" Walt asked. "Maybe I could run you home and then return with the truck."

Roberto appreciated Walt's concern, but he said quickly, "No way. Parker's gonna be hoppin' mad as it is that one of us isn't able to work. He'd go ballistic if *both* of us showed up back at the ranch. Besides, the guys need you to help round up the cattle. Those steers are probably stretched out over thirty acres by now."

"Okay," Walt said, blowing out his lips in frustration as he hoisted his stocky frame back up in the saddle and turned to go. "Well, good luck."

"I think I need something more than luck," Roberto mumbled as he eased his pain-wracked body behind the steering wheel.

It didn't take long for Roberto to realize the ride on Walt's horse had been a piece of cake compared to the lurching of the truck and trailer as they bounced over the uneven dirt roads.

But no one could hear him now, so he gasped and moaned whenever he felt like it—which was just about every few seconds.

Roberto finally pulled into the yard beside the bunkhouse and dragged his aching body into the building and onto his bed. Unfortunately, lying down felt even worse than sitting up.

As he struggled to find a position that might ease the pain, a soft knock sounded on the bunkhouse door. "Come in," he called weakly, knowing that at least it wasn't Mr. Parker. He'd never bother to knock.

The kindly face of their Guatemalan cook appeared around the door. Roberto watched her smile immediately turn to concern when she saw the dried blood on his face. "Señor, qué pasó?" Antonia asked in Spanish, wanting to know what had happened.

Before Roberto could answer, she was rushing over to the tiny kitchen sink. She got a towel wet, then started cleaning the caked blood off his face and hands with a tender, motherly touch.

Roberto wanted to smile at Antonia while she worked, but even that seemed to hurt. He always tried to talk with her when she delivered their lunches and dinners each day, but she usually left quickly, fearing Mr. Parker's wrath if she stayed around too long. In those brief moments, however, Roberto had grown to appreciate and admire this gentle lady. Now, even though he winced every time she dabbed at his wounds, her caring touch felt like the brush of an angel compared to the rest of his life here.

After Roberto briefly explained his accident, Antonia hurried back to the house to get some wide elastic strips made for wrapping hurt ribs. Wisely, she had tucked them away many years ago when Mr. Parker had broken a rib.

"Mr. Parker, he gone to town for business," Antonia said in her version of English while she wrapped Roberto's chest. "He be back for dinner."

Just knowing Mr. Parker was gone made Roberto feel better.

"Please call doctor, señor," Antonia said as she finished securing the strips around him.

He could read the alarm in her dark eyes when he replied, "I can't, Antonia. I've got no insurance or money. And I can guarantee you ol' Parker won't pay."

Antonia shook her head and made a sound under her breath.

Roberto attempted another smile as he gingerly touched her arm. "I'll be okay, Antonia. I'm young. I'll heal fast."

The kind woman nodded and began arranging some pillows on a chair so he could sit more comfortably, then she rushed toward the bunkhouse door. "Must get back to house—Mr. Parker need supper ready," she said over her shoulder as she disappeared out the door.

With the bandage securely fastened around his chest, the pain began to ease a little. But sitting with nothing to do all afternoon gave Roberto time to think—something he normally tried not to do. When his mind could wander, it always seemed to run back to memories of his loving home at the Cassidy Ranch. *What an idiot I've been!* he thought as he pictured some of the fun times he'd had there. Roberto dropped his head and stared absently at the dirty wooden floor. He watched a large cockroach scamper across the far corner. *All those temptations to leave home had looked so great—but look what they turned out to be....*

Roberto discovered that sitting quietly for hours brought another kind of pain. Not only were his memories full of sorrow, but he knew the other three cowboys were out there struggling to regroup the scattered cattle and herd them back to the pens—with one less rider.

Through the grimy window, Roberto saw the last rays of sun dip behind the hills. Then he heard weary-sounding calls from the three cowboys. The bunkhouse shook a little with the pounding of hooves as the herd ran into the holding pens nearby. He also heard the sound of Mr. Parker's massive truck rumbling into the yard not far from the bunkhouse.

Roberto pictured the scene going on just outside his door: Mr. Parker was getting out of his shiny pickup while the tired ranch hands herded the last of the cattle into the dusty stalls. Then Gunny would go over and give his boss a report.

As things quieted down, Roberto overheard their conversation through the flimsy walls of the bunkhouse.

"How'd it go?" Mr. Parker asked.

"Okay, sir," Gunny said, then there was a pause. Roberto knew the foreman was debating whether or not to tell his boss about the stampede incident. Everyone knew Jeremiah Parker tended to get hot under the collar when things didn't go just as planned.

Finally Gunny said, "We got all them cattle outta the back pasture. They's ready to load up for the rodeo t'morrow."

65

"Good, good," came Mr. Parker's reply. Then another pause. "Where's the Mexican?" Roberto could easily imagine the man's narrowed steely eyes and tight lips as he spoke.

"Uh," Gunny said hesitantly, "a branch broke off a one of them big ol' oaks and caused a stampede through the canyon. It spooked Roberto's horse, and the kid got purty banged up by them cows. He got some cuts—maybe some busted ribs." After a moment Gunny added, "He's lucky to be alive."

In the bunkhouse, Roberto held his breath waiting for the explosion from his short-tempered boss...but it didn't come. Mr. Parker merely said, "Just some hurt ribs?"

As Roberto let the air out of his lungs, he thought Mr. Parker sounded rather flippant about an accident that could have killed one of his ranch hands. But, of course, Parker didn't care about anyone but himself, and how things might affect his profits.

Gunny's voice continued. "We think so, sir. Don't rightly know till he's been to see a doctor."

"Doctors," Mr. Parker said, gruffly. "They'd want to run every test they know on the worthless kid just so they could charge me lots of money. Then they'd pat him on the back and tell him it's only a couple a' bruised ribs that'll just have to heal on their own."

Roberto was sure that if Mr. Parker had been a doctor, that's the way *he* would practice medicine.

After a moment of silence, Mr. Parker asked, "How'd he get home?"

"On the back of Walt's horse, then he drove hisself in the

truck," Gunny said, a bit of admiration in his tone.

Roberto could hear the ice in Mr. Parker's voice when he said to his foreman, "If he can ride and drive, then he's not hurt too bad. You tell that lazy, good-for-nothin' kid I want him on that truck tomorrow with those cattle headed for the rodeo. That shouldn't be too hard on his fragile little body. You got me?"

"Yes, sir," Gunny replied so softly that Roberto could barely hear him.

Sitting back in his chair, Roberto clenched his jaw. *How can someone be that cold-hearted?* he thought. *If ever anyone needed the Wizard of Oz to give him a new heart, it would be Jeremiah Parker.*

Roberto tossed and turned most of the night, trying unsuccessfully to find a sleeping position that didn't send pain shooting through his side. All that, however, seemed secondary to the seething resentment he felt toward his cruel boss. Roberto slowly shifted to his back and stared at the bunk above him. *Some day…some day I'm going to get Jeremiah Parker back,* he vowed silently as the root of bitterness poisoned his heart.

When the alarm clock rang, Roberto rolled slowly from his bunk and realized he felt a little better. But he wasn't sure how he'd hold up during the day's work ahead.

Across the room, Gunny was pulling on his jeans. He glanced over at the boy. "Them cuts on yer face look like they's doin' okay, but ya got a hum-dinger of a big ol' purple bruise there on yer cheek." He broke into a grin. "It's such a shame to ding up that purty face."

Roberto wanted to throw his pillow at the foreman, but

today it hurt too much to even *think* about moving that fast.

Walt kindly offered to make breakfast in Roberto's place for that morning, but Buster and Gunny immediately volunteered to take it on since Walt had made breakfast the morning before. Buster bent down near Roberto's ear and whispered, "We cowboys are tough, but *two* days of Walt's cooking could kill anybody."

Roberto slowly got dressed, ate, and made his way out to the holding pen. A semi-trailer had backed into the yard to load up the cattle, and the other three men were herding the cows up the ramp and into the huge rig. Roberto saw Mr. Parker standing with his arms folded, watching them from his front porch not far away. Anger seethed through Roberto again as he reluctantly slid onto the passenger seat of the semi. Once the cattle were all loaded, the driver started the massive diesel engine, and they headed for the rodeo grounds sixty miles away.

As they rumbled up the highway toward Cheyenne, Wyoming, Roberto thought, *Well, if I have to work with hurt ribs, at least a rodeo job isn't too hard. All I have to do is take care of some paperwork for the rental of these cattle and make sure they're cared for at the arena. That shouldn't be too bad.* He also knew they might ask him to help run the cattle chute for the contestants, but he hoped that wouldn't happen. *Even if I do have to help with the chutes,* he thought, *it'll still be lots easier than riding all day, or restringing barbed-wire fences, or digging post holes.*

Once they reached the rodeo grounds, Roberto supervised the unloading of the cattle and was then able to relax. But in the afternoon, the workers called him over to help load cattle in the roping chute. Periodically, the cows would get bunched together in the narrow runway, and he'd have to reach in either with a prod or by hand to reposition them. The worst job, however, occurred when one of the cows got its horns caught in between the metal bars of the chute. The animal wasn't hurt, but it definitely hurt Roberto when he had to twist its horns around to free its head.

Suddenly almost every other cow that entered the chute decided to get its head caught, and each time, Roberto would have to grab its short horns and jerk its head free. And every time he did, the stabbing pain in his side increased.

"Not again!" Roberto mumbled as another cow got caught in the chute. Moving up to reposition the animal, Roberto tried in vain to keep his right arm pinned against his side, while he grabbed the cow's horns with his left hand. But something different happened this time. As he struggled with the stubborn cow, pain enveloped his entire body—then suddenly everything went black.

CHAPTER 8

Katie couldn't breathe as she stared at the mountain lion. Her heartbeat thundered in her ears. *Should I run? Should I scream? Is it going to eat me?* She didn't know what to do!

Turning her head ever so slightly, Katie glanced toward Zack—but what she saw shocked her even further than she already was. Zack was digging his heels into Bucky's side and racing straight at the mountain lion! He grabbed the rope off his saddlehorn and began swinging it wildly above his head, screaming at the top of his lungs!

Katie looked back at the huge golden cat and saw its intense stare break away from her to look instead at the large thing racing toward it, making all sorts of threatening sounds. The mountain lion hesitated for a second, as if it was considering whether or not to attack Zack and Bucky. Then it suddenly swung its agile body around and disappeared into the small grove of trees.

Katie slowly stood upright, her heart still beating a mile a minute as Zack reined in beside her. She anxiously searched the woods for any signs of the animal, and felt like her quivering legs might crumble beneath her.

Panting like he had run instead of Bucky, Zack said, "Wow! That was close! That mountain lion could have been on you in a split second!"

Katie reached over and placed her hand against Bucky's neck to help steady her trembling body. Looking at Zack, she stammered, "D-d-do you th-th-think it would have attacked m-m-me?"

"I don't know," Zack said, shaking his head, "but I'm sure glad we didn't have to find out!"

Still in a state of shock, Katie and Zack didn't say anything else for a moment. Then, as if a light bulb had suddenly gone on, Zack said, "Hey, we've got to tell Dad the mountain lion is still here!"

Glancing past him, Katie said, "But Tango's run off. How can I get back?"

Zack slipped his left boot out of his stirrup and held his hand down to her. "Hop up. We've gotta get home fast!"

Katie lifted her foot into the stirrup, grabbed Zack's hand, and swung up to sit behind him on Bucky's haunches. Zack barely gave her time to get a firm grip on the back of his saddle before wheeling the horse around and breaking into a hard gallop toward the ranch house.

As Zack raced Bucky at breakneck speed through the pasture, Katie had to hang on for dear life. *I feel like a ping pong ball on top of a pogo stick,* she thought as she bounced up and down on the horse's back.

"Hold on!" yelled Zack as they sped across the field.

*What do you **think** I'm trying to do?* Katie muttered to herself, desperately digging her fingernails into the saddle.

Soon they ran past Tango, who had now slowed to a leisurely trot on his way home to his stall. They raced on, flying by the barn and up to the house, where Zack pulled Bucky up short and leaped off, almost in a single motion.

Katie saw Diego jogging toward them looking worried. Zack called out to him, "The cougar just about got Katie!"

"What?" Diego said, his eyes growing wide with alarm. "Are you okay, Miss Katie?" he asked as she slid from Bucky's back.

"I'm okay," Katie answered, still a bit breathless and shaky. "Zack ran up and scared the mountain lion off." As the words came out of her mouth, it hit her—Zack had just saved her life!

Diego turned to Zack. "I'll go get the gun," he said. "You get your father. He's down at the barn."

"Okay." Zack vaulted back onto Bucky and raced back down the road.

In no time at all, Diego and Mr. Cassidy were steering the ranch truck out of the yard, taking the hunting dog, Toby, along in the cab to help flush out the big cat. Zack went with them to show where he and Katie had just been, although Katie heard Mr. Cassidy give him strict instructions to remain in the truck—no matter what.

Katie and Mrs. Cassidy watched the men drive away. When the truck had disappeared down the dirt road, Mrs. Cassidy placed her arm around Katie's shoulder and said, "Let's go in and say a prayer, okay?"

Katie just nodded, suddenly feeling her legs getting weak again.

Once inside the house, Mrs. Cassidy first called the game warden. Then she, Katie, and Anna sat together in the living room to pray.

Katie, on the couch next to Mrs. Cassidy, found her pent-up emotions suddenly exploding in a waterfall of tears. As she buried her face in her hands, she felt Mrs. Cassidy's arms wrap around her and hold her close. Katie laid her head against the woman's shoulder.

"It's okay," Mrs. Cassidy said softly. "You're safe now, Katie. It's okay," she repeated as she stroked Katie's hair and held her tightly. Anna also reached out a delicate hand from her wheelchair and placed it tenderly on Katie's leg. Katie looked at the girl through blurry eyes and could see the concern and compassion on Anna's sweet face.

After a few minutes, when Katie's tears began to subside, Mrs. Cassidy turned toward Anna and reached out her hand. "Why don't we say a prayer for the men's safety, okay?"

Anna nodded vigorously and took her mother's hand. The three lowered their heads and Mrs. Cassidy said, "Lord, we thank You for protecting our precious Katie. And thank You for keeping Zack safe as well. We now ask You to help the men find this mountain lion and be able to tranquilize it. But most of all, please keep Matthew, Zack, and Diego safe. In Jesus' name, amen."

"Amen," echoed Anna quietly. When Katie looked up, she saw the young girl meet her mother's eyes. "They'll be okay, Mama," Anna said.

Mrs. Cassidy gave her daughter's hand a gentle pat.

Since cell phones didn't work out in the fields, Mrs. Cassidy and the girls had no idea what was happening. Every minute felt like an hour as time dragged on. Finally, when Katie started tapping a pencil repeatedly on the coffee table, Mrs. Cassidy said, "How about a lesson in making bread while we wait?"

"Uh…all right," Katie said, not quite sure that sounded like fun. *At least it will keep my mind off the mountain lion. I sure hope they find it!*

After several long hours up to her elbows in bread dough, Katie finally heard a truck coming toward the house. Running over to the window, her heart sank when she saw it was only the game warden pulling into their yard. She and Mrs. Cassidy went outside to greet him, but as they approached his vehicle, they heard the ranch truck rumbling its way up the dirt road.

"Yay!" Katie yelled, turning eager eyes toward the pickup. As it came closer, she strained to see if everyone inside looked okay. She wondered if they'd seen the mountain lion, and a shudder ran through her as she pictured the cat's yellow eyes again.

When the truck drew up near the game warden's vehicle,

Katie heard Mrs. Cassidy breathe a sigh of relief. The two men in the front seat were smiling, and Zack was hanging out the side window waving enthusiastically like a soldier coming home from battle.

The moment they pulled to a stop, Zack jumped out. "We got him! I mean her! We got her! Diego put her out cold with one shot!"

The two men climbed out of the truck behind Zack and explained that they had been able to follow the cat's fresh tracks back up into the trees. Mr. Cassidy had taken Toby around on the far side of the grove, and the dog's furious barking had sent the frightened mountain lion leaping onto a low tree limb. Diego had then gotten a tranquilizer into it on the first shot, and the cat had fallen to the ground and laid still.

"And it's a female," Zack informed the group again. "Maybe she was feeling protective," he added with a shrug.

"Or hungry," Katie said as another shiver ran down her spine.

The men transferred the stunned cat from the ranch truck to a cage on the back of the warden's vehicle. As the game warden secured the door, he said, "We'll take her far away where she can hunt to her heart's content. She won't be bothering you folks anymore."

"Good!" Katie said, leaning against Mrs. Cassidy. The lady immediately placed her arm around Katie's shoulders once again.

At dinner that night, Mr. Cassidy thanked the Lord for protecting them all and for their success in finding the cougar.

As he said "Amen," he looked up at his son. "Zack, in all the hustle and bustle of today, I haven't had time to say how proud I am of you."

Katie glanced at Zack and saw him pause from picking up the platter of roast beef and look up at his father with surprise. Matthew Cassidy continued. "You know, when you ran Bucky toward that mountain lion to scare it away, it could have attacked you, son."

Zack looked puzzled for a second, then said, "Dad, there wasn't time to think. I just saw Katie in trouble, and knew I needed to help."

His father nodded slightly. "I'm proud of you," he said again.

Anna's voice came from the other side of the table. "'Do nothing from selfishness or empty conceit,'" she was saying, "'but with humility of mind regard one another as more important than yourselves.'"

Mrs. Cassidy smiled warmly. "That's good, Anna. A perfect Bible verse for what Zack did." Then Mrs. Cassidy looked at her son. "Do you remember where that verse is located, Zack?"

Katie saw Zack close his eyes, obviously struggling to remember.

Anna waited for a few seconds, then answered, "Philippians two, verse three."

"Thank you, Zack," Mrs. Cassidy quipped, her eyebrows raised over a little smile at her daughter.

Zack's face turned a bit red, but before he could respond,

his father said, "That verse describes you today, Zack. You acted selflessly and thought of Katie's needs above your own."

Zack met his father's eyes. "Thanks, Dad." He glanced sideways at Katie, his face now a bright red.

She smiled to herself as he looked away quickly, grabbed a fork, and begin attacking his pot roast.

"And, Katie," Mr. Cassidy's voice caught her attention, "we're just incredibly grateful you're okay."

"Me too!" she said.

Mr. Cassidy cleared his throat, then said, "Katie." His tone sounded serious. Her eyes locked on his. She could tell she had done something wrong.

"When there's danger around, like a mountain lion, you should never get off your horse," he said. "Your horse can run a whole lot faster than you, and he's a whole lot bigger, too. You should have stayed mounted. Do you understand?"

Katie dropped her eyes. "Yes, sir," she said softly.

Mrs. Cassidy jumped in. "We're not upset with you, Katie," she said. "We just want you to learn from this."

"I have!" she said, shaking her head vigorously. She meant it.

As dinner continued, Katie glanced over at Zack a couple of times. Once when their eyes met, he smiled, then turned his attention back to his plate. *Something's different,* she thought, unable to put it into words. She did notice, however, that suddenly Zack no longer seemed like a rival, but a friend—and that felt good.

Bedtime came none too soon that night, and Katie fell

asleep immediately, worn out from all the tension and excitement of the day. When Mrs. Cassidy knocked on her door the next morning, Katie discovered that Sundays came with a special bonus—an extra hour of sleep!

When she finally showed up for breakfast, Katie's jaw dropped open. On the large wooden dining table sat plates of pancakes, eggs, bacon, sausage, homemade bread, and a huge pitcher of freshly squeezed orange juice. *This isn't breakfast—this is a feast!* "Wow! This is amazing!" she said as she looked over the incredible spread.

Zack ate more than Katie thought was humanly possible. Then when he rose to start clearing the table, Mr. Cassidy announced it was time to get ready for church.

Church? she gulped. *What should I do? Are we supposed to dress up?* She wrinkled her nose at the thought of having to wear a dress. All of a sudden she realized she hadn't even seen any of her skirts or dresses in the closet. Until now, she hadn't missed them. But what if she needed a dress? She bit her lip and wondered what to do.

"Uh…" Katie said hesitantly to Mrs. Cassidy, "what—what should I wear?"

"Clothes," Zack said with a taunting grin.

Well, things are back to normal with him, Katie thought as she made a face back.

"This is a simple country church, Katie," Mrs. Cassidy explained. "There's only one church in our little town, so everyone goes there. And because we're all country folks, no one really dresses up. Just put on some clean jeans or pants—

whichever you'd like."

Katie breathed a sigh of relief. Then when Anna described the pants she would be wearing, Katie decided to put on her nice black ones with her favorite light pink top.

Once they were all ready, Katie climbed into the pickup, and Mr. Cassidy gently lifted Anna onto the seat beside her. Everyone else piled in, and Diego and his wife, Maria, followed in their small truck.

Katie stared out the window as the road to town meandered alongside the gurgling Poudre River. She even spied a white-tailed deer disappearing into the thick pine trees beside the road as they rounded a bend.

Soon they pulled up to a pretty, white-painted building topped with a tall steeple. As they made their way inside, the Cassidys introduced Katie to what felt like a million people. *Isn't this supposed to be a small town?* she thought as she extended her hand to yet another smiling stranger. Behind her, Mrs. Cassidy was saying again, "This is Katie Carlson, a friend who's come to stay with us for a while to help with the horses."

Finally the Cassidys, Katie, Diego, and Maria maneuvered themselves into one of the hard wooden pews. Squirming to get comfortable, Katie wondered if anyone ever brought pillows to sit on. As the service started, she kept a close eye on Zack so she wouldn't do something dumb. But when she saw him staring into space as they sang something from a hardback blue book, she shook her head and thought, *Maybe I'd better watch Mrs. Cassidy or Anna instead.*

Eventually a tall man wearing a black suit walked onto

the platform in front and said he was going to tell them a story from the Bible about a man and his two sons. Katie found herself getting interested when he looked out across the audience, smiled, and said, "Most of us can relate to the challenge of raising children." Lots of heads bobbed in agreement with the man.

Well, I suppose I'm a challenge sometimes, she thought. But *my brothers **sure** are!*

The speaker continued and told them about a boy who had run away from home, spent all the money his father had given him, and then finally had come back home and asked for forgiveness. The man talked about how everyone needs forgiveness from the Lord for their sins, and that without it, we are all separated from God. Katie didn't really understand what most of it meant, but she was definitely curious.

As she was thinking about all this, she suddenly noticed Diego's wife, Maria, crying softly. Diego had his arm around her, holding her close. Mrs. Cassidy, who sat on the other side of Maria, was patting the woman's arm. Katie wondered what had been said that had caused her to cry.

When the church service ended and everyone had filed outside, Katie shuffled her feet while the Cassidys stood around for what seemed like an eternity talking with friends. Zack had run off with two other boys his age, and even Anna was sitting a little ways off in a circle of young girls, all chattering away.

When they finally arrived home for a late lunch, Katie found out that on Sundays, Diego and Maria joined the Cassidys for the afternoon meal. And to Katie's amazement, she found *another* huge spread of food set before them. *I'll bet Zack eats at least half of this himself,* she thought as they all sat down around the expanded wooden table.

Mr. Cassidy turned to Diego. "Would you pray and thank the Lord for all His blessings?" he said, nodding toward his friend.

Diego returned the nod solemnly, and they all bowed their heads. Katie was grateful he prayed in English, because recently he had told her that in his own house, he always prayed in his native Spanish. "I believe God thinks it is the most beautiful language," he had said with a smile. She wasn't sure if he had been teasing her or not.

Katie listened to Diego's prayer as he thanked the Lord again for protecting everyone yesterday, and for all God's wonderful gifts of food and shelter. Then he quietly added, "And please, Padre, bring our son Roberto home soon. Please, Señor, keep him safe wherever he is. Amen."

Katie immediately put two and two together. The sermon had been about a runaway son, and Diego's son was gone. *That* must have been why Maria was crying.

After lunch Zack, Katie, and Anna played games all afternoon, so Katie thought she would be tired by bedtime. But as she lay down to sleep, her mind was overflowing with questions from the past few days. When Mrs. Cassidy came into her room to tell her goodnight, Katie looked up at her and said, "May I ask you a question?"

"Of course!" Mrs. Cassidy said, immediately walking over next to the bed.

Katie thought about her words carefully. "Uh…I've heard a lot about God since coming here. But today at church, that man said some of us might not get to be with Him." She paused for a moment as she thought about her next question, then slowly said, "Mrs. Cassidy, if I had been killed by that mountain lion, where would I be now?"

CHAPTER 9

Mrs. Cassidy sat on the bed near Katie. Curious, Katie watched the woman close her eyes as if she was thinking really hard. When Mrs. Cassidy opened her eyes again, she looked over at Katie and gently smoothed her hair. "Katie, I'm not God," she began. "Only He knows where each person goes when he or she dies." She paused to reach for something resting on the nightstand. "How about if we look at what He wrote to us in His Word?" she said.

In all the excitement of being on the ranch, Katie hadn't even noticed the pretty burgundy-colored book sitting on the table beside her bed. As Mrs. Cassidy picked it up and began thumbing through the pages, Katie asked, "What do you mean by 'His Word'?"

"The Bible is God's letter to us," Mrs. Cassidy said. "He

used men to write down what He wanted to say, so we often call it 'God's Word.' And whatever God says to us, we can *always* trust to be right." She continued turning the pages. "We should base all our decisions on what He tells us in His book, Katie, because we know if God said it, it's right."

When Mrs. Cassidy found what she had been searching for, she read out loud, "'For everyone has sinned; we all fall short of God's glorious standard.'"

Katie frowned slightly. "What does it mean by 'sin'? And what 'standard' is it talking about?"

Their eyes met, and Mrs. Cassidy smiled. "Well, the word *sin* means any disobedience to God. See, God is holy and perfect. But we certainly aren't perfect! We all do wrong things and make wrong choices, don't we?"

Katie slowly nodded her head as she remembered some mean things she'd said to Zack. Then she thought of the time not long ago when she had lied to a friend at school because she hadn't wanted to share her new colored marking pens. And then there was the time she'd pushed a girl and made her fall into a mud puddle. And she got mad at her brothers a lot for leaving her out. *Wow, I'm definitely not perfect!* she thought.

Mrs. Cassidy was saying, "And because God is perfect and we aren't, our disobedience separates us from Him. That's why we don't measure up to God's standard, which is what the pastor was talking about this morning." She paused, then her eyes suddenly brightened as she said, "Katie, you told us your brother Mark plays ice hockey, right?"

Katie nodded.

"Well, it's sort of like if you're playing in a hockey game, and you get sent to the penalty box for doing something wrong in the game," she said. "Except in this case, the penalty box for our sins is permanent, and we're separated from our wonderful God forever."

Katie looked at the ceiling as she tried to absorb all these new things. After a moment, Mrs. Cassidy went on. "But God is so good, Katie. He provided a way so we wouldn't have to be separated from Him. He sent His Son, Jesus Christ, to earth. And Jesus lived a perfect life, without any sin at all."

Katie's eyes widened. "Not even *one* sin?" she asked, realizing how often she was selfish and said things that weren't very nice.

"Not even one," Mrs. Cassidy said. "But some men were very jealous of Him, and they killed Him. Jesus could have stopped them, but He willingly chose to give up His life. And then He came back to life from the dead! God tells us in the Bible that over 500 people saw Him alive again—so we know it really happened."

Katie's eyes stayed glued to Mrs. Cassidy as she asked, "But why *didn't* Jesus stop them from killing Him if He really could?"

"Well, Jesus came from heaven to be a substitute payment for all our sins, so we don't have to be separated from God. It's like He offered to sit in the penalty box for us, so we wouldn't have to take the punishment."

Katie grinned. "I like that part!"

Mrs. Cassidy smiled back. "Yes—but now we each have

a decision to make. We need to receive Jesus' offer for ourselves. It's not enough to just know about Jesus." She began flipping through the Bible again, then stopped and showed the page to Katie. "God tells us here, 'To all who believed Him and accepted Him, He gave the right to become children of God.'"

Mrs. Cassidy gently closed the burgundy book and said, "Katie, in order to be a child of God's, we each need to make a choice. We may know all about Jesus and about His offer to pay that penalty for us, but unless we actually accept that payment for ourselves, it doesn't do us any good. But when we believe in Jesus and receive His offer to take the punishment for our sins, then His Spirit comes to live inside us and make us part of God's family." She pointed to Katie's heart as she said, "You can have Jesus in your life too, Katie."

The girl closed her eyes in concentration for a moment as she thought about all of this. Her family had never talked about God and Jesus like the Cassidys did. But she had never experienced the sort of love she constantly felt here on the ranch, either. The Cassidys had something that drew her heart like a magnet.

"Katie," Mrs. Cassidy said, interrupting her thoughts, "when we have Jesus in our life, then He gives us an amazing promise. He says that when we die, we'll go to be with Him forever."

"Really?"

"That's right," Mrs. Cassidy said. "And that's also the answer to your question about the mountain lion. If you've accepted Jesus' payment for yourself, then you can know that

86

when you die, you will instantly go to live with Him."

Katie's mind raced with all she'd just heard. She knew she did lots of things wrong, and she didn't want to be separated from God because of those things. She wanted to be part of God's family, to know for sure what would happen to her if she died. But this was something she'd never thought about before.

Mrs. Cassidy reached over and placed her hand alongside Katie's cheek. "Do you want to think about all of this for a while?" she asked.

Katie nodded and said, "Thanks, Mrs. Cassidy. It's all new to me—but I think it's really important." After a pause, she added, "Can we talk about it again?"

"Absolutely!" Mrs. Cassidy said. "Nothing is more important than a person's relationship with God."

Mrs. Cassidy stood and set the Bible back on the nightstand. She took a step toward the door, stopped, then turned back to say, "I can't begin to tell you all the wonderful changes Jesus has made in my life, Katie. I used to constantly worry, and even be angry, over Anna's condition. But God has changed that. Now I usually feel at peace, because I can trust that God knows what He's doing. And the same thing has happened to Mr. Cassidy and to Zack."

"Tell me about Zack," Katie said with a grin.

Mrs. Cassidy shook her head slightly as she chuckled. "Funny Zack," she said. "If you think he gives you a hard time now, you should have seen him before he asked Jesus into his life. He always *tried* to be nice to Anna, but he certainly could irritate her. He would pester Toby, too, until the poor dog would run and hide in the barn."

Katie giggled. She had no trouble picturing Zack tormenting the dog.

Mrs. Cassidy switched off the lamp on the nightstand, then started toward the door. "Good night, sweet Katie," she said as she gently pulled the door closed behind her.

Katie burrowed deep into her blankets and smiled as she felt a strange sort of pull in her heart that she didn't know how to express. *There's just something really special here,* she thought. It was quite a while before sleep came as her mind kept replaying their conversation.

At breakfast the next morning, Katie learned she would be going into town with Anna and her mom for the girl's physical therapy appointment. That sounded sort of boring, but this was evidently an important time, because today Anna might try to take a few steps. From what they'd said, Katie knew these sessions could be quite painful—but Anna didn't ever seem to complain.

Once the two girls were settled in the truck, Mrs. Cassidy drove them along the sparkling Poudre River until they reached the edge of their small rural town. Katie glanced over to see Anna staring out the truck window as they drove past a fairground.

"Look, Mama!" she said suddenly, pointing toward the arena. "That girl over there is riding her horse and carrying a big flag."

Her mother glanced over quickly and nodded. "She must ride with the equestrian drill team that practices there every

Sunday afternoon."

"Uh huh," Anna said, her eyes glued to the girl as they drove past.

Katie had read about drill teams in one of her many horse books and thought they sounded like a lot of fun. She was getting ready to ask if they ever went to watch the practice, when at that moment Anna turned quickly toward her mother. Anna's entire face lit up as she exclaimed, "Maybe Katie could ride Tango with them!"

"Really?" Katie asked, adrenaline surging through her as the idea sunk in. "Oh my gosh, oh my gosh, that would be so amazing!" she said, shaking her hands excitedly.

Mrs. Cassidy smiled. "Well…" she said, pausing for what seemed like an eternity to Katie.

"Can I? Can I?" Katie begged.

"May I," Mrs. Cassidy corrected her, then said to her daughter, "I hadn't thought about that idea before, Anna. It's a possibility, but we'll have to talk to your dad when we get home. And, Katie, we don't know if there's even a space open on the team for you to be included, so try not to get your hopes up too high."

"Oh, that would be *awesome!*" Katie said a little softer, still so wound up she could hardly sit still.

Upon reaching the doctor's office, Katie jumped out while Mrs. Cassidy put Anna in her chair and wheeled her toward the front door of the doctors' building. As they started to enter, a young man emerged, hobbling on crutches. A thick plaster cast engulfed his entire right leg up to his thigh. Katie saw him meet

Anna's sympathetic eyes. He broke into a grin, looked down at his cast, and said to her, "And I only came here with an ingrown toenail!"

Katie and Anna both hesitated for a second, then broke into laughter as they caught the joke. Mrs. Cassidy smiled at the young man, and it looked to Katie like she seemed grateful to him for bringing a special moment of happiness to her daughter's limited life.

Katie followed along as Mrs. Cassidy moved Anna into a large physical therapy room at the back of the doctors' offices. Soon a smiling, young-looking woman wearing a white medical jacket over her broad shoulders appeared through the doorway on the opposite side. "Hello, Anna," she called, waving her hand.

"Hi, Miss Davis," Anna said, returning her wave.

The therapist strode over to Anna and knelt down on one knee so she was eye to eye with her patient. "And how are you today?" she asked, her voice upbeat.

"I'm wonderful!" Anna said, her blue eyes dancing.

Katie watched as Miss Davis glanced up toward Mrs. Cassidy with an expression of curiosity, then looked back at the girl. "And what makes you so happy today, Anna?"

The girl swiveled in her chair and pointed toward Katie. "Katie's here riding my horse, getting him ready for me. He's beautiful, and Katie's the best!"

A wave of conflicting feelings filled Katie's heart as she tried to smile at the therapist. *"Getting him ready for me..."* repeated over and over in her mind.

Miss Davis rose to her feet as Mrs. Cassidy introduced

her to Katie, then caught the physical therapist up with all the recent events at the ranch. Katie's heart sank even further when Mrs. Cassidy concluded by saying, "So Anna's excited and eager to begin riding Tango when the right time comes."

Miss Davis nodded and looked at her patient. "I'm looking forward to that too," she said, placing a gentle hand on Anna's shoulder. "Riding will be so good for strengthening your core muscles and for your balance, Anna. It should actually help all your other movements too, as well as get you outside and around the ranch more."

Katie looked out the far window. *I know riding will be good for her,* she thought, *and I want Anna to get better. I really do. But why can't she ride another horse, like maybe Bucky?*

Anna's voice interrupted Katie's thoughts. "But I don't know for sure when I'll ride yet," she was saying to the therapist. "Katie will let me know when Tango's ready and the time's right. I trust her." Anna reached over and took Katie's hand.

Katie gave the tiny hand a slight squeeze, then looked away to try and hide her feelings of frustration and confusion.

As Anna's therapy session progressed, Miss Davis soon had the girl standing between parallel bars. Katie found herself cheering Anna on as the girl struggled to take some steps while holding herself up on the bars. By the end of the session, Anna was completely worn out from the enormous effort, so she slept most of the way home. Katie and Mrs. Cassidy rode in silence, not wanting to wake her up.

When they reached the ranch house, Katie downed a quick lunch, then raced to the barn to saddle Tango. She was glad Zack hadn't arrived at the barn yet so she could talk to her horse. "Hey, fella," she said as she set a saddle pad on his back, "did you know you're what I've wanted my whole life?"

Tango turned his head to look at her, almost like he could understand what she was telling him.

She stopped adjusting the pad and met his gaze. "Tango, even if I could, I don't want to go back home yet," she said. "I love it here. I love Mr. and Mrs. Cassidy, and Zack's okay—but I love *you* the most!" Katie threw her arms around his neck and buried her face in his soft mane. "How can I ever give you up?" she whispered.

The moment those words came out of her mouth, a picture of Anna's angelic face popped into her mind, and the all-too-familiar conflict swept over her like a flood. Katie squeezed her eyes shut, desperately wanting to make this horrible dilemma disappear. "I *don't want to* give you up!" she said softly but fiercely to the horse.

"Ready to check out a new trail?"

Katie jerked her head around. Zack's voice had startled her, and she hoped he hadn't heard her words. "Uh…yeah, absolutely—as long as there aren't any mountain lions."

Zack didn't answer but just met her eyes and smiled.

Once they had their horses saddled, the two directed their mounts down the dirt road, into the pasture and through the grove of old oak trees to the left. As they wound their way around the majestic trunks, Katie was amazed at the size and beauty of these silent giants. *This could be an enchanted forest,* she thought, her fertile imagination taking over. She saw herself as part of Robin Hood's gang, jousting with lances, and fleeing through the woods on Tango from the Nottingham sheriff.

Emerging from the grove, Zack led them into the pasture of Jersey cattle where they'd been before. As he closed the gate behind them, Katie saw him look at her with a mischievous expression. But before she could ask what was going on, Zack dug his heels into Bucky's side, yelled "Yah!" and burst into a gallop across the field.

Katie immediately took up the challenge and spurred Tango in close pursuit. *No boy's going to outrun me!*

Startled cattle scattered right and left as the two riders flew through the herd and raced across the field. Katie bent low over Tango's neck, urging him on with her hands and legs. His flowing mane blew into her face as he pounded across the ground and quickly caught up with Bucky. Little by little Tango overtook Zack's horse by a nose, then by a neck.

The path abruptly veered to the left, and Zack turned with it. But because Katie didn't know the trails, she was a second late in guiding Tango through the turn. Bucky easily leaped out in front again, and before Tango could catch them, the pasture fence brought their race to an end.

As Katie and Zack pulled the animals to a stop, both horses snorted hard, their nostrils flaring wide and red. Katie moved Tango alongside Bucky while she panted for breath and started laughing all at the same time. "You cheated! We had you, and you cheated!"

"Did not! We beat you fair and square!"

"I didn't know the trail, so it wasn't fair!"

"Ignorance is no excuse," Zack declared, a huge grin splitting his face. As their eyes met, he shrugged slightly and added, "Well, that's what Dad always says, anyway."

In response, Katie reached over and punched his arm. But this punch wasn't like when they'd first met. She couldn't put it into words, but it felt like some kind of bond was growing between them, and only a friendly sort of whack could really convey her feelings.

As they rode on past towering pine trees and across rolling hillsides, Katie noticed how Tango was becoming so much easier to handle—which made her heart extremely heavy again. She turned her face away from Zack so he wouldn't see her expression. Her mind churned as she reached down to stroke the horse's warm neck. *Mr. Gateman said my job was to prepare you for Anna. But you know how much I want to keep riding you. Yet…how can I be so selfish to sweet Anna?* Katie let out a long sigh. *What am I going to do, Tango?*

While Katie silently struggled with her feelings, Zack led them through a gate she'd never seen before. As they walked toward the far side of this field, a steady roaring sound grew in their ears. Cresting a hill, Katie suddenly saw a fast-flowing river thirty feet below them, glistened with varying shades of blue in the afternoon sun. White foam swirled in areas where the water rushed over large rocks and boulders. As their horses began to carefully wind their way down the slick, muddy path toward the water, Katie shook her head in awe at the gorgeous sight.

Once they reached the bottom of the hill, they turned onto a narrow bank that ran alongside the river. Rocks and an occasional poplar tree lined the stream's shoreline. Zack dismounted and tied Bucky's reins to a tree close by, so Katie did the same.

For a few minutes, the two stood quietly at the edge of the river, taking in the beauty of the crystal blue water as it rushed down the creek bed toward the Cassidy's lake below. Katie sighed again. This was all so perfect!

Zack turned to her and pointed up and to the left. "See those mountains up there?"

Katie nodded, her gaze falling on the jagged peaks standing starkly against the light blue sky.

"In the winter," Zack said, "those mountains are covered with snow. Then in the spring when the snow melts, we get all this water."

Katie listened quietly as Zack went on. "Some people waste water and don't realize its incredible value. But without it, this ranch couldn't exist. We need it, the cattle need it, the grass needs it, our crops need it—everything. So we try not to waste it."

Zack's solemn face quickly changed as he leaped up on a large boulder that stuck out into the stream. Katie watched him stand there like King of the Ranch as he spread his arms wide and said, "This is one of my favorite spots. The melting snow right now makes this section of the river the deepest. See how much darker blue the water is here than farther upstream?" he said, pointing to the deep section just beyond the boulder.

Katie nodded, noticing that the water seemed to remain dark blue for a long way downstream.

Zack said, "Dad and I have been fishing here a couple of times this year already."

"Catch anything?"

"Yeah, a couple of really great fish. We took them home to Mom for dinner." He smiled. "Of course she made Dad clean them. You know, slimy fish guts and all."

Katie rolled her eyes. *Some things just never change.*

Zack grinned, his freckles and red hair highlighted by the bright afternoon sun. He then turned around on the rock, bent down, and leaned over to search the clear blue depths for fish.

All of a sudden, his feet began to slip on the wet rock. Katie watched helplessly as he flailed his arms in an attempt to regain his balance, but before she could even move, he fell head first into the rushing water!

"Zack!" Katie screamed. From where she stood, it looked like he had struck his head on a large rock in the riverbed when he fell. She watched in horror as his body was instantly swept downstream!

CHAPTER 10

Katie could only see Zack for a few seconds in the rushing water before he disappeared around a bend in the river. But it looked like he may have finally gotten his head above the surface again. Katie, however, quickly lost sight of him.

What should I do? Frantically her eyes swept around the area and fell on the horses tied to a nearby tree. Rushing over, she ripped Tango's reins loose from the branch, grabbed Zack's rope off his saddlehorn, and turned Bucky loose. She didn't know if she could handle a rope or not, but she needed to throw something in the water to Zack.

Katie leaped onto Tango in a single motion and wheeled him around. As he burst forward in a pounding gallop along the riverbank, she thought, *If I can just get past Zack and somehow arrange the rope for him to grab, maybe that will work.*

But…do I know how to do that?

Racing next to the shoreline, Katie spied Zack bobbing in the water ahead. *At least he's able to breathe!* She saw him try to grab a large rock in the middle of the stream, but his hands merely slid off the slippery surface. She also noticed that none of the tree limbs hung low enough for him to reach. *I've got to get far enough ahead of him so I have time to do something with the rope!*

Once Tango had galloped a ways beyond Zack, Katie pulled the horse to a stop. Holding Zack's rope in her hand, she jumped to the ground and glanced around quickly. On the opposite bank of the river sat a big, smooth boulder. *Here goes nothing,* she thought as she began circling the rope over her head like she'd seen cowboys do in the movies. With a mighty heave she sent the loop flying about twenty feet across the river—and it landed perfectly over the boulder and slid around it to the ground!

Katie could see Zack continually trying to grab things as he floated toward her. She knew that if he took hold of the rope now, it could slip up and over the rock, leaving her hanging on to one end while Zack pulled on the other. *I'm not strong enough to hold him!* she realized in a panic. *I've got to get my end tied to something before he sails past me. And he's almost here!*

With lightning speed, Katie pulled the rope as tight as she could around the bottom of the boulder, then attached her end to the base of a tree on the riverbank near her. The instant she had the rope secured just inches above the surface of the water, Zack reached it.

The force of his body against the rope immediately caused it to slip off the smooth boulder. Katie glanced anxiously at the tree trunk beside her, but her knot held fast. "Yes!" she shouted as Zack began pulling himself over toward shore. Katie's excitement faded, however, when she noticed Zack grimacing every time he tried to use his right arm.

When he finally dragged himself within reach, Katie helped him onto the bank and asked, "What's wrong with your arm?" She also saw a small gash on his forehead.

"I'm f-f-f-f-freezing!" was all Zack could manage to say. His entire body was shaking uncontrollably.

Katie sprang into action again. Pulling Tango alongside Zack, she said, "We've got to get you home fast!" She helped push him onto the back of the horse, then quickly mounted and began the ascent up the steep riverbank. Calling over her shoulder, she asked, "Can you hold on, or are you shaking too badly?"

"I'm ok-k-kay," he said, barely able to get the words out.

Now she was *really* worried. He could hardly talk! Not knowing what else to do as Tango picked his way up the slippery hill, Katie began to pray silently. *God, if You can hear me, please help Zack. Please help him stay on the back of Tango until we can get home. Please help him be okay, God.*

It seemed like it took forever to reach the top of the slope, but once they did, Katie moved Tango into a gentle lope, and Zack wrapped his good arm around her waist. She remembered how hard it had been to hang on with *two* hands during her frightening trip on the back of Bucky, and Zack only had *one* hand he could use, so she didn't dare go any faster.

Since she couldn't see how Zack was doing, and he didn't say a word the whole way home, Katie anxiously chewed on her lip. But when she pulled Tango up beside the back door and slid off to help Zack down, he stammered, "I c-c-can d-d-do it mys-s-self!"

Katie dropped her arms and gave him a quick glare. "Well, obviously you're not hurt *too* badly."

As Zack landed on his feet, Mr. Cassidy came running up from the barn. When he got near them, Katie saw him glance from her to his wet, shivering boy. "Fall in the river, son?" he asked. Katie could see the concern on his face.

"Y-y-yes s-s-sir," Zack answered.

"Let's get you inside," Matthew Cassidy said, slipping his arm around Zack as he quickly ushered the boy into the house.

After taking Tango to the barn, Katie hurried back to the house and stood in the corner of the living room, waiting nervously while the house buzzed with activity. She could hear Mr. and Mrs. Cassidys' anxious voices in Zack's room as they got him into warm clothes. Anna waited in the hallway, her face paler than usual.

When they all returned to the living room, Mrs. Cassidy bundled Zack in a blanket on the sofa and began cleaning the cut on his face. "Not too bad," she said soothingly, putting a small bandage on his forehead.

Mr. Cassidy wrapped Zack's wrist with some elastic tape, then went to make a doctor's appointment. Mrs. Cassidy disappeared for a minute, returning with a hairdryer that she started using on Zack's mop of damp hair. Even their hunting dog, Toby, came over and laid his silky brown head in Zack's lap as if to offer his body heat to the boy.

"I'll make some hot chocolate!" Katie volunteered, wanting to be useful.

"That would be great, honey," Mrs. Cassidy said, not taking her eyes off her son. "That should help get Zack warmed up."

Katie ran to the kitchen to heat up cups of hot chocolate for everyone. While she worked she overhead the conversation in the living room. Zack told them how he'd slipped off the rock and gone headfirst into the freezing water. "I put my hand out so I wouldn't hit a rock," he was saying, "but I hit the bottom pretty hard. I think maybe my arm is broken."

"I got you an appointment with the doctor first thing tomorrow morning," Mr. Cassidy said, returning to the room after making his phone call. "Or do you think we should run you to the emergency room in Fort Collins right now?"

"No, Dad, that's too far." Zack held his injured arm up slightly. "It already feels lots better with the tape around it."

Just as Katie brought the mugs of hot chocolate on a tray to the living room, Anna said to her brother, "So tell us how you got out of the river."

Zack turned to look at Katie, so she related the entire story to them, ending with, "Then I threw him the rope."

Zack's green eyes instantly got really wide. "Wait a minute," he said, "didn't you have that rope over a boulder on the other side? How'd you do that?"

Everyone turned to stare at Katie.

Oh no! she thought. *Here we go again. What do I say? I didn't even know I could throw a rope like that!*

Mr. Cassidy must have seen her hesitation, because he came to her rescue. "Our Katie is just full of surprising talents. That was evidently some pretty impressive rope work, little lady."

Mrs. Cassidy's voice choked a bit as she said softly, "Thank you for helping Zack, sweetheart."

Katie looked down at the carpet and said slowly, "Well… he saved my life, so…" she glanced over at Zack, "I guess we're sort of even now, huh?"

Zack's eyebrows shot up. She could read his face. He had liked saving her life…but to have a *girl* save his? His reaction made her want to giggle. As their eyes met, however, Zack's expression changed. He looked down briefly, then up at her again and smiled slightly. "Thanks, Kate," he said softly.

That made *her* eyebrows shoot up with surprise—he really meant it! Katie returned his smile, and at that moment she knew their friendship was settled once and for all.

At dinner that evening, Katie didn't say much, but mostly listened as Mr. and Mrs. Cassidy kept saying how grateful they were to God for saving Zack's life and for giving Katie the level-headedness to help him. Several times she and Zack glanced at each other and smiled or chuckled a little. One time she felt her face turning red, so she quickly looked away. *I'm sure glad he's okay,* she thought. *Actually, he is kinda cute.*

As Katie climbed into bed that night, Mrs. Cassidy came into her room and sat beside her. Katie wasn't quite ready to go to sleep yet, and she pulled back just a little when Mrs. Cassidy leaned over to give her a goodnight hug. Quickly she asked, "Mrs. Cassidy, do you remember our conversation last night?"

"Of course I do," she said with a smile.

Katie met her eyes, grateful that Mrs. Cassidy was always so available to talk. "Well," Katie said, "I prayed for Zack as we were riding home today. I was afraid he was really hurt, and I couldn't do much to help him. So I prayed to God."

Mrs. Cassidy nodded. "And did He answer your prayer?"

Katie thought about it and at that moment realized God *had* answered her prayer. Zack had stayed on the back of Tango, he had made it home, and he was going to be fine. "He did!" she replied.

Mrs. Cassidy brushed Katie's hair back from her face and said, "God loves for us to pray, and He loves to answer prayers." She paused, then asked gently, "And have you thought any more about your question of what happens to us when we die?"

Katie nodded slowly, then all of a sudden she felt as if a light bulb had just been switched on inside her head. "Wow!" she said, "we never know when we might die, huh? I mean, it could have happened to me with the mountain lion, or Zack in the river! We just don't know for sure—any of us at any time!"

"That's true," Mrs. Cassidy said. "Only God knows how many days we each have—and He doesn't tell us." She waited for a moment, as if to let that thought sink in, then said, "And what does that make you think, Katie?"

Without hesitation Katie blurted out, "I want to know where I'm going if I die!"

Mrs. Cassidy smiled and reached over for the Bible on the nightstand. "Do you remember what we looked at in this book?" she asked.

"I think so," Katie said, watching Mrs. Cassidy thumb through the pages.

When Mrs. Cassidy found the place she was searching for, she put her finger on a verse and turned the book so Katie could read it too. "God promises each one of us here in the book of Romans that 'if you confess with your mouth that Jesus is Lord and believe in your heart that God raised him from the dead, you will be saved.'"

"Saved?" Katie asked.

"It means saved from that separation we talked about last night. Remember?"

Katie nodded. "Oh yeah, because God's perfect and we're not, so we have to sit in the penalty box."

"That's right," Mrs. Cassidy said. "Or we can accept Jesus' substitute payment as our own and let Him take the penalty for us." After a pause, Mrs. Cassidy said, "Katie, do you want to ask Jesus into your life and live with Him forever?"

"Yes!" Katie scrambled up from her pillow. She wasn't sure she totally understood all of this, but she had no doubt that she said and did lots of wrong things. And she *really* wanted to know for sure what would happen to her if some animal decided to have her for lunch. "What do I do?" Katie asked eagerly.

"Well, you tell Jesus you believe in Him, and you accept His offer to pay for your sins. It's as easy as that," Mrs. Cassidy said as she took Katie's hand into her own. "You can close your eyes and pray that right now if you want—either silently or out loud, it doesn't matter which."

"I'll pray out loud," Katie said with a serious face, "…so I'm sure He hears me."

Not really knowing anything about how grown-ups did it when they prayed, Katie closed her eyes and simply said from her heart, "Dear Jesus, I *do* believe in You, and I thank You for Your offer to pay the penalty for all my sins and mistakes. I know I do lots of stuff I shouldn't, so I receive Your payment for all those things. And I ask You to come into my life so I can be with You forever—especially if a mountain lion eats me. Okay, uh…amen."

Mrs. Cassidy bent down and engulfed Katie in a warm hug. "That's the most important decision you'll ever make in your life," she said, squeezing the girl tightly. "I'm so happy for you."

Katie didn't know what to expect after saying that prayer, but all at once she felt a warmth and happiness inside her that wasn't like anything she'd ever experienced before. She readily returned Mrs. Cassidy's hug, and wanted to jump out of bed and hug everyone else in the house too. *Well, maybe not Zack,* she thought with a smile. *I could just give him a punch on the arm.*

Mrs. Cassidy sat back a little and said, "Oh Katie, you are a joy. You certainly are transparent—I can see you're excited."

"I've never felt like this before!" Katie exclaimed.

"Well, the important thing is not the feelings," Mrs. Cassidy said as she stood up, "but knowing that God always keeps His promises. We'll chat more about it all later, okay?"

"Okay," Katie said, laying back on the pillow. As Mrs. Cassidy bent down and pulled the covers up around her neck, Katie gazed into the woman's loving eyes. "Thank you, Mrs. Cassidy," she said. "Thanks *so much!*"

Katie lay in bed, far too excited to fall asleep. She felt like her heart was overflowing with a new kind of love for others, and the only way she could explain it was that she felt less concerned about herself and more concerned about them. Also, for the first time since arriving at the ranch, she wondered if her absence was causing her parents to worry. She hadn't even stopped to consider how anxious they might be about her. She'd only been thinking about how much fun *she* was having. *I hope Mr. Gateman is taking care of that, somehow,* she thought.

As her mind turned to the Cassidys and how much she loved them and loved being at their ranch, something began happening in her heart. *Maybe I **could** give Tango to Anna,* she thought. *I mean, there's got to be another horse I could ride, right? Or I could ride Blaze or Bucky. At least I'd still get to be on this amazing ranch.* Slowly her mind drifted into the most peaceful sleep she had ever experienced.

When Katie awoke the next morning, she felt like she was seeing life through new eyes. She couldn't explain it, but things were just *different.*

When Katie appeared for breakfast, she found a note saying Mrs. Cassidy and Anna had taken Zack to the doctor's office. As she poured a bowl of cereal and sat down at the table, Mr. Cassidy came in the kitchen and sat across from her. Katie looked up, wondering if he had something he wanted to tell her.

"Katie," he said, "Mrs. Cassidy and I have been talking about you riding Tango with the local equestrian drill team."

Katie immediately stopped chewing and dropped her spoon.

"I gave the manager a call, and it turns out that a spot has just come open on the team," he said. "They actually need someone immediately. So if you want, you can practice with them this coming Sunday afternoon. Are you interested?"

"Interested?!" Katie almost shouted, then slapped her hand over her mouth when she realized it was still full of cereal.

Mr. Cassidy smiled. "You'll need to learn the routine quickly, because the team will be performing at the Larimer County Rodeo the following weekend. Are you up for that?"

Katie swallowed quickly. "Totally!" she said, jumping to her feet.

Mr. Cassidy also stood up. As he did, Mrs. Cassidy appeared through the doorway, wheeling Anna before her. Zack followed, and Katie couldn't read his expression. "Are you okay?" she asked.

Zack nodded. "Yeah, I have a sprained wrist, but no broken bones."

Katie said, "That's *good* news, right?"

Zack bumped his tennis shoe against the table leg a couple of times. "Well…the doctor told Mom that I can still do most of my chores."

Everyone laughed, and Mr. Cassidy said, "I'm glad you're okay, son." He patted Zack's shoulder and headed out the door.

The rest of the week sped by. Katie continued to work Tango, noticing how every day he was becoming easier to ride and handle. Her love for the Cassidys and Anna also grew each day, along with her attachment to Tango. On the days she worked him in the ring, Mrs. Cassidy would bring Anna out to watch. She would lean forward, hold onto the wooden rails, and often giggle or clap her hands in delight, which only increased Katie's mixed feelings. She knew that sometime soon she was going to have to tell them Tango was ready for the young girl—and one part of her was happy about that. Another part, however, just didn't want to give him up.

When Sunday finally came, Katie found it really hard to sit still during church and lunch. All she could think about was getting to ride with the drill team. She felt like it took *forever* to get Tango loaded into the horse trailer and for everyone to pile into the truck and drive to the arena.

Once there, she helped Mr. Cassidy unload the horse while Mrs. Cassidy wheeled Anna over to the grandstand to watch the rehearsal. Katie had to smile when she noticed Zack desperately looking around, evidently searching for at least *one* other boy who might be there. When he didn't find anyone, Katie saw him shuffle slowly toward the stands behind his mom and sister, obviously embarrassed at being the only boy present at a *girls'* event.

Katie was adjusting Tango's saddle when a teenage girl appeared beside her on a spotted grey horse. Katie soon learned her name was Meg.

"So you're going to take Sara's place, huh?" Meg asked.

"I don't know," Katie shrugged. "What did Sara do? I've never ridden on a drill team before."

Meg's mouth dropped open. "Really?" she said. "Sara was an end rider. That's an important and dangerous spot on the team." She paused, as if to give dramatic weight to her words, then said, "Sara was really good, but last week while riding in that position, she fell off and hurt her arm. I guess that's your spot now." Then Meg shook her head and muttered more to herself than to Katie, "You've never ridden with a drill team before, and you're bringing up the tail. Wow."

Katie looked up at Meg. "What do you mean?" she asked, starting to chew on her lip with worry.

"Uh…" Meg hesitated, "nothing." She quickly turned her horse to leave as she called out, "I'm sure you'll do great. It was nice to meet you, Katie."

Katie looked around. Mr. Cassidy had gone to sit in the grandstand with his family, and she didn't know anyone else she could talk to about this scary situation. Besides, she really needed to get Tango warmed up before the practice began.

As Katie rode her horse into the arena, she clutched the reins tightly with one hand while she chewed on the fingernails of her other hand. Tango snorted and tossed his head, sensing her nervousness.

"Line up!" called the announcer through the loudspeaker on the tall booth at the front of the arena. An older teenager, who appeared to be captain of the drill team, rode up to Katie and directed her to a spot at the end of the drill line. "I heard you've never done this before," she said matter-of-factly. She looked Katie over from top to bottom, then said, "Just follow the horse and rider in front of you and do what they do. And… good luck." The girl whirled her horse around sharply and loped back to her position in the front.

Katie swallowed hard. *I guess Meg said I was "bringing up the tail" because I'm at the end,* she thought. *But why does everyone make it sound so dangerous?* Just then, twangy western music blared through the loudspeakers, the drill team began their maneuvers…and instantly Katie understood everyone's alarming comments.

CHAPTER 11

Roberto was slowly regaining consciousness, and the first thing he became fully aware of was the fiery pain throughout his entire side. He groaned, feeling like a hot branding iron was pressing against his ribs. He opened his eyes and found himself staring up into the concerned face of a middle-aged cowboy kneeling in the dirt beside him. Other curious faces peered at him from above.

"Easy there," the man near him said, his voice low and quiet.

"Not again," mumbled Roberto. "What happened?"

"You blacked out," the man said. "I was on my horse waiting for the chute to open, and when it didn't, I saw you lying there in a heap. I checked your vital signs, and your pulse seems okay. Do you know what's wrong?"

Roberto stared up at the man. "You a doctor?" he finally asked, barely above a whisper.

The man smiled. "Well, I used to be. I turned in my stethoscope for a rope a couple of years ago, but they still call me 'Doc' around here." He paused, then asked again, "So…do you know what made you black out?"

"Hurt ribs, maybe broken," Roberto said weakly.

The doctor nodded. "That would certainly explain your moaning when we tried to pick you up while you were still unconscious." He glanced around, then looked back at the young man. "Do you think you can walk over to that bench?" he asked, motioning toward a seat near the cattle pens.

Every fiber of Roberto's body screamed that he didn't want to move an inch, but with cowboy courage he bravely said, "Okay, Doc."

The cowboy doctor looked up at the faces around them and said, "Thanks, guys. I'll take it from here."

As the small crowd dispersed, Roberto let Doc help him to his feet. The pair slowly made their way over to the bench, and Roberto eased himself down on the hard seat.

After sitting for a while, the pain began to subside. Roberto filled the kind doctor in on the series of events that had led up to his collapse. He thought he saw the doctor grimace at the mention of Jeremiah Parker's name.

When Roberto had finished his story, Doc sat down on the bench too and looked at Roberto with sympathy. "Son, I've discovered that cowboys are a tough breed," he began. "So many of you are held together with pins and metal plates, you could set off an airport security alarm twenty feet away. But a body can take only so much, and you no doubt were simply overcome with the pain from your injured ribs. You shouldn't ever have been sent out here to work today. And you need an X-ray to see what's really happened inside. Then you've got to get some bed rest to give those ribs time to heal."

Roberto nodded. He knew all that—but what could he do? "Sorry. Can't," he stated simply. "I don't have any money for medical help, and Parker for sure won't pay." Roberto's eyes narrowed as he said, "Mr. Parker told me this injury was *my* fault for being careless." Instantly he felt the desire for revenge flood his heart again.

Doc shook his head. "This just isn't right," he said with a sigh. "I wish there was something I could do, but I retired two years ago to pursue this crazy horse passion, and I don't have my equipment anymore."

They sat in silence for a few minutes, then Roberto saw the doc's face suddenly light up. The man jumped to his feet. "Roberto, let me help you walk over to my truck," he said, motioning toward the parking lot, "because I can take you to a nearby clinic where we can get you an X-ray for free. A friend of mine is there today, donating his time, and he won't charge you." Then Doc added with a wink, "Besides, he owes me a few favors."

The rest of the afternoon, Roberto received the thorough medical attention he so badly needed. The X-rays showed that he did indeed have three cracked ribs. At the end of his examinations, Doc offered to drive him back to Parker Ranch.

On the way to the ranch, Doc said to Roberto, "I hope I run into Jeremiah Parker so I can give him a piece of my mind."

Roberto smiled slightly. "It'd be even better if you just ran into him with this truck."

Doc laughed. But when he dropped Roberto off at the bunkhouse, Mr. Parker was nowhere to be seen.

Grateful that the following day was Sunday, Roberto finally had a full day to rest and recuperate. But come Monday, Jeremiah Parker once again demanded that he rise with the others and do some work around the ranch. Gunny, however, protected him as much as possible, and the three ranch hands often took over some of Roberto's tasks when Mr. Parker wasn't around.

All that week, Roberto eagerly looked forward to the upcoming weekend. He had been promised a long-awaited two days off, and he sure needed the extended rest for his aching body. Usually he could hitch a ride into town with one of the guys and spend the day away from the ranch at a local hangout. *Simply being away from Parker Ranch should help me heal faster than any medicine,* he thought.

Friday afternoon, Roberto whistled softly while he stood outside the barn washing horses. It had been a long day of rounding up cattle for another weekend rodeo. When he saw Mr. Parker's shadow near him, however, he went silent.

"Kid!" yelled the man.

At the sound of that voice, anger and hatred immediately filled Roberto's heart. He turned very slowly toward his boss, setting cold, loathing eyes on the large man.

Their eyes locked, and an evil look crossed Mr. Parker's

face as he said, "Tomorrow you'll go out with the cattle to the Loveland rodeo. Gunny has all the paperwork you'll need." He turned sharply on his heel to walk away.

Without even thinking, Roberto clenched his fists and yelled, "No!"

Mr. Parker whirled around to glare at him. "What did you just say to me?" he hissed.

Roberto's anger exploded. "You're a mean-hearted snake! You know I'm off this weekend—unless of course your word means as much as this pile," Roberto yelled, pointing to a fresh mound of manure.

Jeremiah Parker took a few threatening steps toward the young man. In a low, deliberate tone he said, "No one talks to me like that." Roberto could see him flexing his hands into fists.

Roberto squared his shoulders and tightened his hands into powerful knots. *I might have some aching ribs, but that old man can't begin to match me in a fist fight,* he thought, actually eager for that first swing.

Adrenaline pumped through Roberto as he watched Jeremiah Parker slowly take a deep breath, relax his hands, and stand up tall. A wicked smile crossed the man's face, and his eyes narrowed to thin slits. "Let's get this clear, kid," he said through clenched teeth. "Either you're on that truck tomorrow, or you'll never set foot on this ranch again. Or any other ranch, for that matter—I'll see to that. You got me, *boy*?" He whirled around and marched toward the ranch house.

Roberto's heart pounded furiously in his chest as he watched Mr. Parker's arrogant stride. *Just wait, Parker. Just wait.*

My time will come, and you'll wish you'd never met me. Just wait.

As Katie and Tango began the drill team routine, Katie quickly discovered that being the "end rider" meant your horse raced through most of the drill at a full-on gallop in order to stay in position. The farther down the line you rode, the faster the pace became—and she was the tail.

The team moved into a Flying "V" formation, and Katie reined Tango to the far outside, making sure she remained even with the other tail rider in the pattern. Then when each horse reached the end of the arena, they turned around quickly and switched into a Flying Cross, where the two lines crisscrossed through each other at a fast pace.

For the horse and rider at the tail, each turn and maneuver taken at such breakneck speed meant the horse's feet could easily slip out from under it, or the rider could lose her balance and fall. But Tango kept his footing, and Katie stuck to him like glue.

With the girls working in near-perfect unity, the drill team transformed into a fascinating sight of varying patterns executed with perfect precision and timing. Each formation was like a dance, and sometimes it seemed as if the horses even knew how to keep time with the music blaring from the arena loudspeakers. Straight lines melted into tight circles. Flying Vs shifted into springs that wound tightly, then miraculously unwound and ended up as straight lines again. All the while, the two team captains led the way, one carrying a brightly colored flag with the Red Spangled Drill Team logo, the other carrying the stars and stripes.

Once in a while, the riders would stop to regroup or to receive coaching from the man in the grandstand booth. When the girls halted to hear his instructions, their horses' sides would heave mightily as they tried to catch their breath. Tango's nostrils flared bright red with every great intake of air, since he and the other end-position horse had to run far harder than all the others. Katie kept reaching down and patting his neck, white with lathered sweat. She was so proud of her horse!

In final preparation for their performance next week, the coach called the team to regroup one last time for a run-through of the entire program. Tango put his head down, dug into the soft arena dirt, and executed the routine perfectly.

As soon as the rehearsal ended, Meg rode over to Katie. "You did *great!*" she said, a big smile on her face. "I'm so glad it worked out for you to join us. We'd sure be in trouble if it weren't for you."

Although Katie was panting a little from the exertion and excitement, she grinned from ear to ear. "Thanks! Yeah, Tango and I had a lot of fun." She patted her horse's sweaty neck again and said, "I just had to trust him to keep his footing, and he did."

"Well," Meg said, "all the girls are saying what an amazing job you did, and they're really glad you're riding with us."

Just then several girls rode by and called out, "Good job!" to Katie.

Katie felt like she'd never been happier. Just when it seemed like things couldn't have gotten any better, something even *more* fun had happened!

After cooling Tango down a little, Katie rode back to the trailer, dismounted, and took off his saddle. "You were *awesome,* Tango," she said, starting to scrape the lather off his body. "Way to go, fella."

Katie turned to pick up a brush, but was startled when she saw Zack standing behind her. "Oh! Where'd you come from?"

Zack looked down and began digging his toe in the dirt. Finally Katie said, "What?"

"Uh—," Zack said hesitantly, looking up, "uh…that was actually pretty cool."

Katie's jaw just about hit the ground. *Wow, that's a **huge** compliment coming from him!* she thought. "Thanks," she said, ducking behind Tango so he wouldn't see her enormous smile.

As Katie started to walk Tango around the arena for a final cool-down, the smile just wouldn't leave her face—until she glanced over toward the grandstand. There sat Anna, grinning and waving happily with all her energy. Katie gave a small wave back, but seeing the girl was like suddenly having a giant pin jammed into her balloon of excitement. Looking at Anna brought back the painful reminder that she was going to have to turn Tango over to the girl soon.

Staring absently at the arena sand underneath her feet, Katie continued to walk Tango. *As life with the Cassidys gets better and better,* she thought, *this decision just gets harder and harder. And besides that, there's something else Mr. Gateman hasn't even told me yet.…*

CHAPTER 12

"Here you go, boy," Katie said to Tango, hanging a brimming water bucket in the front corner of his stall. She was thankful for the time alone in the barn with her horse after returning from the practice session at the arena. Tango stretched his neck forward toward the pail, and Katie reached out to rub his velvet nose.

With a loud snort, Tango suddenly backed away a few steps. His ears pricked forward, and his wide eyes stared at something behind Katie.

Katie turned to follow his gaze—then gasped and leaped backwards! For a split second she froze, then placed a hand over her pounding heart, looked crossly at the large figure standing right outside the stall, and said, "Stop doing that!"

Mr. Gateman smiled. "Sorry, little lady. I didn't mean to

startle you."

Katie's mouth curled. "Uh huh," she muttered a bit sarcastically.

"Well, Katie," he said, his eyes seeming to study her, "it looks like you're enjoying your time here."

Katie couldn't stay cross. "This is a dream come true!" she said as she reached an arm under Tango's neck. The horse pressed his face up against her cheek.

"I'm glad you're having fun," Mr. Gateman said. "And do you remember I told you that you'd been brought here for a purpose?"

Katie sighed, looked down and pushed at some straw with the toe of her boot. "Yes," she said softly. She could feel the big man's dark eyes boring into the top of her head, but she didn't want to look at him. When he didn't say anything, however, she finally glanced up and said, "Yeah, I'm getting Tango ready for Anna."

Mr. Gateman nodded, his Panama hat bobbing up and down in approval. "Good, Katie. Good."

She swallowed hard as she made a decision. She couldn't stand the curiosity any longer. "Uh...you said last time that there was something else. Can you tell me yet?" She wasn't sure she really wanted to know, but *not* knowing was even worse.

"Yes, now is the time," he said solemnly. Mr. Gateman stepped through the stall door and placed a hand on her shoulder. "Katie," he said, looking into her eyes, "I told you before that you would learn something very important here. And you know it's up to you when Anna rides Tango."

Katie nodded. "I know," she said quietly, waiting for more.

Mr. Gateman continued. "But what you don't know is that once you give Tango to Anna, your part here is completed."

Katie gasped. *Completed? Like, finished? Meaning I have to leave Tango AND the ranch?* She felt like she'd been flattened by a bolt of lightning.

Katie felt tears beginning to well up in her eyes, so she twisted away from Mr. Gateman's hand and took a step back. She looked toward Tango and asked in a choked voice, "Will I ever come back?"

Mr. Gateman sounded almost fatherly as he said, "No, Katie. But there are other adventures just as great waiting for you. To experience them, however, you will need to make the right choice here."

"I don't want other adventures," she said, barely above a whisper. A big teardrop hit the stable floor. "I want this one." She tried to wipe her eyes with her hand, but she couldn't stop the flow of tears. She felt like she'd been stabbed in the heart.

Katie stared at the floor as she ran a hand over her face again, creating long streaks of dirt down her cheeks. Finally she lifted her eyes—Mr. Gateman was gone! Turning back toward Tango, Katie buried her face in his soft mane and released an avalanche of tears. For a time, no sound could be heard in the barn except for her heartbroken sobs.

When her tears finally stopped, Katie stepped over to Tango's water bucket and splashed some cold water on her face. She then slid down the side of his stall and sat in the hay. Holding her head in her hands, she tried not to cry again. She was sure her eyes were puffy and wanted them to return to normal before anybody saw her.

Tango dropped his head and pushed his nose gently against her hair. Katie reached up to touch him. "It just keeps getting worse, fella," she said hoarsely, rubbing his nose. "I'd gotten to where I thought I could give you up to Anna…but now I have to give up *everything*—and never even see you again." Her voice caught, and it felt like the tears might start all over.

Katie didn't know how long she sat on the floor of the stall, but finally she rose slowly to her feet with a long, drawn-out sigh. "I'd better get to the house before they wonder what's happened to me," she said, giving Tango's neck a loving pat.

After slowly closing the horse's stall door, Katie started toward the house. Her steps dragged all the way up the road. *I just went from one of the best moments of my life to one of the worst—and now I've got to act like everything is fine.*

Katie's life at Cassidy Ranch had begun to fall into a routine. She started each day with early morning chores, followed by a wonderful breakfast. Then she would either work Tango in the ring—under Anna's delighted gaze—or ride out in the fields. Zack would go with her on rides through the pastures, and they would usually make up some Wild West adventure as they loped around the cattle herds and up and down the hills. They had so much fun together—yet Katie could never completely ignore the decision that hung over her like a nasty black cloud.

Toward the end of that week Zack and Katie were pretending to herd the cattle away from evil rustlers who were trying to steal them from the ranch. In the middle of the game, Katie suddenly stopped under a large oak tree.

"Hey!" Zack yelled, "they're getting away! You can't quit now! What kind of deputy sheriff are you?"

Katie jumped off Tango and called to Zack, "Sorry. My saddle's a little loose." She flipped the stirrup up out of the way and began tightening the cinch strap. "I guess the bad guys will have to win today," she added with a smile.

"No way!" Zack said. "We'll just say they're frozen for now, okay?"

Katie nodded and continued to adjust the cinch as Zack rode over. "This is great!" he said, looking toward the cattle, then back at her. "I've never had a friend around every day like this. And we can do this the whole rest of the summer!"

Her hands froze on the strap. Zack seemed to notice the change, because he looked at her with a frown. "What? What'd I say?"

Katie shook her head. She knew Zack couldn't figure out why she'd suddenly become quiet, but what could she tell him? Feeling a confusing mixture of happiness because of their friendship, and sadness because of her future, she said slowly, "Zack, if some day soon I have to leave, I just want you to know that…well…." She wasn't quite sure how to say what she felt in her heart.

Zack looked puzzled. "What do you mean?"

Katie smiled and said softly, "I just wanted to say that— well, you'll always be my best friend."

For a second Zack looked completely befuddled, but Katie

was sure she also saw him smile a little. His face, however, instantly turned bright red as he fidgeted with Bucky's reins and looked away. "Yeah, uh, okay," he mumbled and gave Katie a fleeting glance. He then wheeled Bucky around hard and rode off toward the imaginary cattle rustlers.

When Saturday finally rolled around—the big day of Katie's performance with the equestrian team—she came bounding out of her room, almost running headlong into Mr. Cassidy. "Whoa there," he said with a smile as he caught her in his arms. "Not excited about the drill team, are you?"

"When do we leave?" she asked. "Do I have time for breakfast?"

Mr. Cassidy chuckled. "We don't need to leave till after lunch," he said. "That should get you there in plenty of time to warm up Tango before the drill team opens the rodeo." Then he stopped. "But, Katie, I'm not going to be able to take you. I've got some work here I simply have to stay and do. Diego is going to drive you and the family to the arena."

Katie smiled and nodded. "That's okay. But I'm sorry you don't get to come."

"Me too," he said, returning her smile. "You and Tango looked great with the team, and I loved seeing Anna's face as she watched her 'big sister' ride her horse."

Katie's smile faded, and she turned away toward the kitchen.

Time seemed to almost stand still that morning. Katie tried to stay busy in the barn with chores and brushing Tango down for the event. When lunchtime finally came, she practically inhaled her food, then ran outside to help Diego attach the horse trailer to the truck. She wasn't very good at signaling Diego correctly as he tried to back the truck up to the right spot, but after several tries they finally had the trailer's hitch over the truck's ball.

Katie began apologizing to Diego for her poor directions, but he smiled, waved his hand, and said with a laugh, "It's okay, Miss Katie. My son Roberto, he's no good at directions either. One night, he almost ran me into the barn!"

Katie laughed too. But as she looked at the kind ranch hand and thought about his missing son, she turned serious and said, "I'm sorry you don't know where Roberto is, Diego. I know that must be hard."

Diego turned away for a moment, and to Katie it looked like he was searching the horizon for his son. When he turned back to her, his eyes brimmed with tears. Softly he said, "Maria and I, we miss our son very much. We pray God keeps him safe."

"I'll pray that too," Katie said, feeling a depth of concern for them she'd never felt for anyone before.

Soon everything was ready to go. Once Mrs. Cassidy had Anna settled in the truck, the rest of them hopped in. Driving away, they all waved to Mr. Cassidy and Zack. Katie had been disappointed when she'd learned that Zack wasn't going to see her ride either, but Mr. Cassidy had said he really needed the boy to help him with some of the ranch work that afternoon.

As they made their way toward the city, Katie felt like Diego was driving less than ten miles an hour. Finally she turned to him and asked as sweetly as she could, "Diego, how much farther?"

Mrs. Cassidy smiled. "Diego, I think someone is *really* eager to get there."

"Sí, sí," Diego said with a grin. Katie's fidgeting and loud sighs had been hard not to miss. "Not far now, Miss Katie," he said.

After what seemed like forever, they finally pulled into the Larimer County fairgrounds beside several other horse trailers. Mrs. Cassidy and Anna headed for the grandstands while Katie and Diego got Tango out and ready to go. Katie had borrowed an official outfit from the girl who had gotten hurt, and when she saw the reflection of her sparkling, red sequined jacket in the truck window, she stood up tall.

Meg brought her horse over while Katie finished brushing Tango. The other girl was chattering on about horses and riding with the drill team when suddenly she stopped in mid-sentence. Katie turned as she heard Meg whistle softly and say in a hushed, excited tone, "Look over there!" Meg pointed in the direction of some men standing a short distance away by the cattle pens.

Katie followed Meg's gaze, but she couldn't see anything particularly fascinating. "What?"

"There!" Meg pointed again. "That gorgeous guy in the black hat!"

Katie looked again, then smiled when she saw the young man Meg seemed so excited about. Katie wasn't boy-crazy yet, but she had to admit, that guy really was good looking. "Yeah," she nodded, "he *is* cute."

Diego joined the two girls from the other side of the trailer. When Katie saw his grin, she could tell he'd overheard their conversation. "Not saddled yet, Miss Katie?" he teased, then turned to see what they'd been looking at.

Suddenly Diego gasped!

Katie stared at him with alarm—his face had turned pale, and his mouth gaped open. "Diego?" Katie said urgently, "Diego, what's wrong?"

But he didn't answer. He just stood frozen, as still as a marble statue.

CHAPTER 13

Roberto and the other ranch hands beside the cow pen continued their conversation, completely unaware of what was happening over by the horse trailers. One of the cowboys gnawed on a toothpick stuck in the corner of his mouth. He said to Roberto, "I heard Doc Mason had to pick you up outta the dirt t'other day."

Roberto smiled and nodded, dropping his head so his large cowboy hat almost concealed his eyes. "Got some cracked ribs," he said, pushing at a dried cow chip with his boot. "But ol' Parker still made me work that rodeo last weekend. The pain got pretty bad."

"Good thing you're young and heal fast," the cowboy said.

An older ranch hand from a Wyoming outfit piped up beside Roberto. "Yeah, good thing, 'cause if you were out of circulation, who would all them young girls look at?" He chuckled as he nodded toward Meg and Katie.

Roberto shook his head. "What are you talkin' about, Sam?" he asked, turning to follow the man's gaze. Roberto saw the girls—then suddenly inhaled sharply.

"Papá!" Instantly joy, fear, and apprehension swept over him like a giant wave.

The moment Roberto's eyes met his father's, Diego took a hesitant step forward.

Roberto's heart pounded in his ears, and he no longer heard the men around him. As he brushed past one of them and began walking slowly toward his father, his mind raced with every step. *Will he hate me? Will he ever be able to forgive me? How can I tell him about all the awful things I've done? Will he ever trust me again?*

As the two drew closer, Roberto completely forgot the pain in his side and broke into a run, quickly covering the remaining steps between them. When he reached his father and saw only tender compassion in his eyes, Roberto threw his arms around him and let the tears flow. Diego held him close.

"Lo siento, Papá! Lo siento mucho!" Roberto choked out, saying he was so sorry. "Please forgive me." Roberto didn't know what his father would say, but at that moment it didn't matter. He had to plead for forgiveness—he couldn't live like this any longer.

Diego took a step back from Roberto and held his son's face in his calloused hands. Their eyes locked, and Diego said in a voice breaking with emotion, "Mi hijo!" *My son!* "Of course

I forgive you." Then Diego again wrapped his arms around Roberto's neck, continuing to whisper, "Mi hijo, mi hijo."

Roberto and his father finally began walking over toward the Cassidy trailer. When Roberto noticed the two girls—who had obviously been watching the entire reunion—he quickly tried to dry his face on his shirt sleeve.

Diego introduced his son to Katie and Meg, and Katie joyfully shook Roberto's hand. Roberto could tell, however, she wasn't quite sure what to say at this emotional moment. And she must have realized Diego needed time with his son, because Katie turned to Meg and said, "We should go warm up our horses," motioning toward the arena.

"Uh…oh! Okay," Meg said.

"We'll see you later," Katie called over her shoulder as the girls led their horses away.

Finally alone, Roberto sat in the truck and told Diego all about his miserable past two years, continually asking his father for forgiveness. Each time, Diego reassured his son of his unwavering love, regardless of the boy's bad choices.

A voice boomed over the loudspeaker: "Ladies and gentlemen, let's give a warm welcome to the Red Spangled Drill Team!" The crowd stood to their feet, clapping and cheering as the girls and their mounts streamed into the arena. Their sequined jackets sparkled in the afternoon sun as the riders followed their two flag-bearing captains around the ring. Katie smiled when she spied Mrs. Cassidy and Anna out of the corner of her eye as she swept past the bleachers. *This is so incredible! I can't believe*

I'm here! On Tango! She tried to keep her excitement in check while the drill team worked through their maneuvers perfectly.

The dazzling routine came to an end all too soon, and the girls filed out the gate at the far end of the show grounds. As they brought their horses to a stop, Katie leaped off Tango and asked Meg to hold him while she ran up to the grandstands. Rushing over toward Mrs. Cassidy and Anna, Katie began calling out over all the noise, "Roberto's been found! He's over there with Diego!" she said, waving her arm toward the trailer.

Mrs. Cassidy stood to her feet, a hand shading her eyes. "Really?"

"He's in the truck!" Katie hollered. "Come on!"

Katie could see that Mrs. Cassidy's eyes were filled with tears as she pushed Anna's wheelchair as fast as she could toward the truck and trailer. "This is certainly more important than any old rodeo!" Katie heard her say to her daughter, who was clapping her hands in excitement.

When the three reached the truck, Roberto stepped out. Katie noticed that Roberto looked both happy and sorrowful at the same time. Mrs. Cassidy rushed to him and embraced him in one of her loving hugs.

Katie saw Roberto grimace slightly, and Mrs. Cassidy quickly pulled back and looked at him with questioning eyes.

"Cracked ribs," he said, in answer to her puzzled expression. He smiled a little and added, "But when I'm healed, I want to make up for all the hugs I've been missing these past two years, okay?"

Mrs. Cassidy nodded, unable to speak as the tears flowed

down her face. Katie remembered Mrs. Cassidy saying that Roberto's smile could light up a room—but it looked like it had been a long time since he'd had much to smile about.

Katie went to retrieve Tango from Meg, then cooled her horse down and brought him back to the trailer for a good brushing. As she started to comb out his forelock, she overheard Diego ask his son if he wanted to go home with them. She turned to peek at the two men and saw Roberto drop his head. "If you'll have me back, Papá, I want to go home with all my heart," she overheard Roberto say. Katie turned back to her horse, grinning from ear to ear as Diego reassured his son how very much they wanted him home.

Once Tango was loaded into the trailer, they all piled into the truck and drove out the fairground gate. Katie saw Diego glance at his son sitting beside him on the front seat. "Is there anything you need to get from la hacienda del Señor Parker?" Diego asked him.

At the mere mention of Jeremiah Parker's name, Katie saw the blackness that clouded Roberto's face. He said through a clenched jaw, "No. I don't *ever* want to see that place again as long as I live."

Katie watched Diego and Mrs. Cassidy exchange a meaningful look. She could read the concern in their eyes. Something was festering inside Roberto that shouldn't be there.

When they arrived at the ranch, Maria couldn't stop crying and laughing and giving her son hugs—"...but I do not hug so hard to hurt the ribs," she said. Then once her tears finally dried, she flew into action. A spontaneous "welcome home" party began. Zack and Mr. Cassidy set up several tables outside. Katie chuckled as she watched Maria emerge over and over again carrying plates and bowls piled high with tortillas and salsa, burritos, taquitos, and anything else she could find in her house. It was especially funny when Mrs. Cassidy playfully held Maria so she couldn't run back to her kitchen for any more food.

In the following days, Katie noticed how life at the Cassidy Ranch took on a "new normal." Roberto began to help his father with easy chores, and Maria continually clucked over him like a mother hen, constantly worrying about how he was healing. Katie rode Tango daily, knowing with an unbearably heavy heart that the time had come—he was ready for Anna.

One sunny afternoon, a few days after Roberto's homecoming, Katie was brushing Tango in the barn following a good workout. Roberto appeared in the doorway and smiled at her, making her feel self-conscious and her face grow warm. She accidently dropped the horse brush with a loud clatter on the barn floor. As she hurried to pick it up, a bit more red crept into her cheeks.

"Tango looks really good," Roberto said, obviously trying to put her at ease.

"He's an incredible horse," Katie replied, running the brush over the horse's dark chestnut haunches again.

"That's one good thing I did have at Parker's place—a decent horse," Roberto said, a far-away look coming into his eyes.

Katie hesitated before asking, "Was it really terrible there?"

She watched as anger suddenly transformed Roberto's face. It reminded her of how the tide reveals all sorts of things on the shore after it recedes into the ocean.

When Roberto spoke, his voice sounded icy and cold. "You have no idea," he said, shaking his head. "Jeremiah Parker is an evil, despicable snake."

Katie wasn't sure how to respond, but Roberto didn't give her a chance. He narrowed his eyes and said, "That man made my life miserable. He'd dream up ways to torture me, then *laugh* about it." Roberto paused and turned to stare out the barn doorway. Katie saw him clench his fists and heard him say under his breath, "I've been waiting to get even with him for a long time."

She shifted uncomfortably for what seemed like forever. Finally, she noticed Roberto drop his eyes and relax his hands. She saw a puzzled frown cross his face as he said slowly, "But I don't know...." His voice trailed off, and it looked like he was struggling with something inside.

Katie bit her lip, desperately wanting to change the subject. She attempted a smile and said with forced cheerfulness, "Well, uh, everyone sure is glad to have you back! Your mom and dad were awfully worried about you."

Roberto raised his head slowly. Katie was surprised at how sad he looked. He said softly, "Yeah, I don't deserve the parents God gave me, Katie. I know I've hurt them, and I'd do anything to make it up to them." He gazed out the barn door again as he thought for a moment, then added, "I don't deserve their forgiveness—but I'm sure glad I got it."

Katie exclaimed, "Oh, guess what! I got *God's* forgiveness last week! I asked Jesus to come into my life and pay for all the bad stuff I've done. That's pretty awesome!"

Roberto looked like he froze in place. Katie could see he was thinking, and when he spoke again, each word sounded very deliberate. "That's great, Katie," he said. "I asked Jesus into my life when I was about your age, too. I'd been sort of a mean kid before that," he said with a little smile, "so I really remember what it felt like to have God's forgiveness."

Roberto paused, and his face grew serious again as he said quietly, "I knew I didn't deserve God's forgiveness. And now my mom and dad have forgiven me, and I don't deserve that either."

As they stood in silence, Katie could tell the wheels in Roberto's mind were spinning. She didn't know if she should say anything or not.

Suddenly Roberto looked at her with intensity. "Katie, do you know what anger and bitterness do to your heart?"

She shook her head. *What a strange question,* she thought. *No one has ever asked me something like that before.*

Roberto continued. "They're like poison. They eat away at your heart until there's nothing left." Then as if speaking to himself, he said softly, "It looks like that's what happened to me. I've let bitterness toward Jeremiah Parker eat away at my heart."

Katie wasn't sure what to do or say. But as she watched Roberto, she saw something happening. It was like seeing the sun start to peak out from behind a black cloud. The hard expression on his face began to soften.

"You know what, Katie?" he said in a much gentler voice.

135

She shook her head again.

"You've reminded me that I don't deserve all the tons of forgiveness *I've* gotten," Roberto said, "so who am I to not forgive Jeremiah Parker?" Roberto dropped his head again and stared at the dirt floor.

For a few seconds, the only sound was the occasional swish of Tango's long tail. Finally Roberto nodded a little, as if to himself, then he looked up. With a slight smile and a voice so soft she could barely hear him, he said, "Gracias, Katie. Thanks." He turned and slowly walked out of the barn.

As Katie watched him go, she realized she'd been holding her breath. With a long exhale, she thought about what had just happened. *When Roberto forgave his awful boss, it looked like he also let go of a bunch of anger and bitterness. He looked...well, peaceful. Wow, I think I got to see God do something pretty amazing!* She couldn't help but smile as she turned back to Tango.

But her smile didn't last long. When she remembered her own situation and what loomed before her, Katie sighed and dropped her head against Tango's neck. *What am I going to do?* she mourned.

"Hey!" Zack's voice from the barn doorway made her jump and whirl around. "I just passed Roberto, and he looked really happy," Zack said. Katie could see the mischievous sparkle in his green eyes as he went on. "So...I guess you guys were in here talking, huh? Got a new boyfriend?"

Katie shook the wooden-handled horse brush at him. "Zack Cassidy, you take that back!"

Zack quickly raised his arms over his head. "Okay, okay,

I take it back!" he said, then muttered to himself, "A little touchy, aren't we?"

Actually, she was feeling a little touchy. Mentioning to Roberto how worried his parents had been brought to mind her own parents, along with her selfishness in wanting to stay here. Were her mom and dad worried about her, just like Diego and Maria had been for Roberto? And what about her selfishness toward sweet Anna? Katie's dilemma began to eat at her again. *Tango's ready. Anna's ready,* she thought to herself. *Am I ready?*

Meeting Zack's eyes, Katie said softly, "I'm sorry, Zack. I guess I've got something on my mind."

Zack grinned back. "That's okay. Sorry to tease you. That was kinda mean."

Katie's eyes got really big. *Did Zack Cassidy just apologize to me?* She shook her head. *Amazing things **are** happening around here!*

Then it hit her like a bolt of lightning. *God isn't just working on Roberto's heart. And He isn't just working on Zack's heart. He's working on **my** heart too!*

She suddenly looked at Zack. "Is Anna in the house?" she asked urgently.

"Yeah. What—?"

But Katie was flying past him on a dead run toward the ranch house!

CHAPTER 14

As Katie raced toward the house, she heard Zack yelling, "What? What'd I say?" But Katie's mind was elsewhere.

She burst through the back door, practically falling head first over Toby. Running into the living room, she saw Anna sitting calmly in her wheelchair beside the coffee table, working on a jigsaw puzzle. She could hear Mrs. Cassidy clattering dishes in the kitchen. Katie looked at the girl and blurted out, "Anna, do you want to ride Tango now?"

"N-n-n-now?" Anna stammered, her wide eyes looking both surprised and excited.

Mrs. Cassidy immediately appeared at the living room doorway. "Katie?" The one word conveyed many unspoken questions.

Katie breathlessly continued. "Right now!" she said

emphatically with a big, encouraging smile. Then she paused for a second. "If you want to, of course."

Anna began to bounce up and down. "Yes! Yes! I want to ride Tango!" She quickly looked at her mother. "Is it okay, Mama? Can I ride him now?" With pleading eyes she added, "Please, Mama?"

Katie could read in Mrs. Cassidy's face the desire to protect her daughter and concern about putting her on top of a powerful horse. But as Mrs. Cassidy looked back and forth between the two girls, Katie thought to herself, *It almost looks like she knows what's been going on in my heart!*

Mrs. Cassidy finally smiled at her daughter's imploring eyes and nodded. "Okay, honey. I think it's the right time. But let's make sure your father thinks so too."

"I'll go round everyone up!" Katie said, whirling around and racing back out the door to get Mr. Cassidy, Zack, and Diego's family for this important event.

As Katie began gathering the group together, she thought about how this moment in her own life was far bigger than any of them knew. But she kept that to herself as she directed them toward the horse ring without telling them exactly why, then returned to the barn and began saddling Tango again.

Setting the saddle on the horse's back, Katie stopped for a moment, then spontaneously threw her arms around his neck like she'd done so many times these past few weeks. Only this time was different. This might be the *last* time! Pressing her face against his silky mane, she said softly, "I love you so much, Tango. I don't *want* to leave you. But I can't keep you any longer."

Katie moved around to face the big horse and gaze into his eyes. With tears starting to trickle down her cheeks, she took his velvety muzzle into her hands and said, "You be good to Anna, okay? No fast turns or anything. You have to take care of her." The words caught in her throat as she whispered, "She needs you more than I do."

Burying her face into his mane again, Katie wept—but this time her tears were not from frustration or pain. She noticed with surprise that in an odd sort of way, it actually felt *good* to take something that meant so incredibly much to her, and give it up to someone who needed it even more. She'd never felt like this before. She knew her decision also meant she would be leaving the ranch soon. But her tears of sadness over saying goodbye to this horse and the people she loved so dearly were mixed with tears of joy over being able to give something very precious to a frail little girl.

After drying her eyes, Katie finished saddling Tango. As she led him toward the ring, she looked at each person assembled there. Mrs. Cassidy must have gotten an okay from her husband, because there sat sweet Anna, squirming eagerly in her wheelchair, proudly decked out in a fringed cowgirl shirt, new jeans, and shiny blue boots.

Katie stopped Tango inside the arena, and Mr. Cassidy scooped up his daughter in his arms and carried her into the ring. Turning to the group, he said in a rather loud, formal tone, "We're all assembled here this afternoon to witness a very important occasion." As he gently lifted Anna up into the saddle, there was lots of clapping and oohs and aahs. Then Mr. Cassidy told Anna to hold on to the saddlehorn while he and Katie shortened the stirrups.

Katie watched Tango's face while all this was happening. She had heard that horses have a unique sense about the people riding them. They know when someone can ride, when someone feels fearful, and when someone needs their help. Katie could tell from Tango's eyes—somehow he knew the instant Anna landed in the saddle that this fragile person required special care.

When Katie handed the reins to Anna, Tango stood perfectly still. It was as if he instinctively felt a sort of protection over his precious passenger and didn't want to make a move that would startle or injure her.

Anna carefully held the reins while Katie attached a lead rope to Tango's bridle. Katie gave the girl a few basic instructions, then began leading them around the ring. As they walked past all the cheering onlookers, Katie noticed there wasn't a dry eye among them. Even Zack looked kind of emotional.

For half an hour Katie walked Tango and Anna around the corral, periodically stopping to teach her a new riding skill. She showed Anna how to rein left and right and how to stop and back up. Katie quickly discovered that Anna's keen eyes had been absorbing a lot more about proper riding technique than Katie had realized. And every time Anna practiced something different, she practically squealed with delight. Katie had never seen the girl happier than at this moment.

Mr. Cassidy finally called to his jubilant daughter, "Okay, honey. I think we'd better stop for today. You don't want to wear Tango out so he's too tired to take you riding tomorrow, do you?"

he said with a grin.

"Oh, Daddy," Anna giggled.

Katie looked up at the girl. "Okay," she said, "you know how to rein Tango over to the fence and cluck at him softly to start walking. Show 'em how it's done." Katie released her lead rope from the horse's bridle and let Anna go on her own, merely walking alongside them.

Anna turned the horse toward her family and friends and gave a soft clucking sound. Tango seemed to step very carefully as he took her over to the fence, then stopped when she reined him in.

"Perfect!" Katie said, smiling up at Anna. Katie laid her hand tenderly on the girl's thin leg and looked up into her beaming face. "He's all yours, Anna," she said softly, then turned away quickly as she felt tears welling up in her eyes.

Mr. Cassidy came into the arena, slid Anna down from the saddle, and carried her back to her wheelchair outside the fence. As he set her down in the chair, Katie heard him say, "That's my girl! Great job, honey."

While everyone gathered around Anna, ecstatic over this big step in her life, Katie stood in the ring alone, holding Tango. She happened to glance over at Zack, and when their eyes met, he climbed over the wooden fence and walked up to her. "Thanks, Kate," he said, punching her lightly on the arm. "That meant a lot to my sister."

Katie nodded. Her heart felt like such a jumble of emotions right now, she was afraid to speak. She just stared down at the sand in the ring.

"Something wrong?" Zack asked.

"No," Katie answered quietly. "No, everything is right." She gave him a slight smile and added, "But thanks. Thanks for everything, Zack."

Before he could respond, she began leading Tango out of the ring toward the barn. After a few steps, she glanced around and saw Zack still standing there, watching her. Then she heard his mom calling, "Zack, will you push Anna back up to the house? I have something I need to do."

"Sure, Mom," Zack said. "It'll be an honor to help the best little rider on the ranch."

Once Tango was in the barn, Katie removed his bridle and slipped a soft rope halter over his head. Lost in thought, she was surprised to hear Mrs. Cassidy say, "Katie," right behind her.

"Oh! Hi!" she said. "Sorry—didn't know you were there."

Mrs. Cassidy smiled and stretched out her arms. Katie immediately flew across the space between them, snuggling close to this woman she had come to love.

"Katie," Mrs. Cassidy said, "thank you for what you've done for Anna—and for our whole family." She ran a loving hand over Katie's hair.

"What do you mean?" Katie asked. *What have I done for any of you?*

As if reading her mind, Mrs. Cassidy held her close and said, "Well, you've worked Tango until he was ready for Anna, you've been a wonderful big sister to her, and you've been a great friend to Zack. And you've brought a lot of joy and laughter to our home."

Katie pulled back just enough to look at her. "Thanks," she said, "but you've given me more than I can even begin to tell you." She stopped as she felt a lump growing in her throat. *I don't want to cry!* she thought, glancing away quickly.

Mrs. Cassidy released the girl and held out something in her hand. "We have a gift for you, Katie."

"A gift?"

Katie watched as Mrs. Cassidy placed a small, burgundy leather book into her hand. Then she looked up into the woman's eyes.

"It's a pocket Bible," Mrs. Cassidy said. "We want it to remind you of us wherever you may be."

Katie thought something in Mrs. Cassidy's voice almost sounded like she already knew about the girl's upcoming departure. *I don't want to think about that yet,* Katie said to herself as she looked at the beautiful little Bible in her hand. She immediately felt more tears starting to spill down her cheeks. "Thanks," was all she could choke out. She continued gazing at the book and finally managed to whisper, "Make sure everyone knows how much I love them, okay?"

Mrs. Cassidy nodded and placed a tender hand on Katie's face. "Our sweet Katie," she said, then turned and headed back to the house.

Katie could hardly see the small book in her hand through her blurry eyes. Her heart felt like it might explode with all the love she had both received and felt for this family. And then there was Tango, a horse she adored far more than she ever thought was possible.

Carefully placing the Bible into her back pocket, Katie turned to the horse. Removing his saddle, she began brushing him with long, loving strokes.

Suddenly she noticed a shadowy figure standing at the far end of the barn. She studied the shape, then said in a low voice, "Mr. Gateman!"

When the large man stepped out of the dim light, Katie could see the smile creasing his wide face. "Well, Katie," he said, "you did it."

Katie nodded slowly. "You know what?" she said softly, "it actually felt good to give Tango to Anna."

"I'm proud of you," Mr. Gateman said, bobbing his head and Panama hat up and down. "Very proud."

Katie smiled. But when she glanced toward her beloved horse, she felt a knot in her throat. "When do I have to leave?" she asked in a whisper, reaching out to rub Tango's neck. Before she could touch him, however, an odd sensation swept through her body. At first it felt like a giant vacuum sweeper pulling on her. Then her entire body seemed to stretch like a giant rubber band!

Katie quickly realized what was happening and desperately tried to touch Tango one last time.

CHAPTER 15

Katie reached toward Tango with all her might, but her fingers couldn't feel him! Then, as the barn began to whirl around her like a tornado, she could barely even *see* him! *Here we go again!* she thought as everything became a complete blur. Katie got so dizzy she wasn't sure if the things around her were spinning or if *she* was the one spinning.

With no sense of space or time, Katie felt like the whirling lasted forever, until she finally landed on something soft. "Ugh!" she moaned, putting her hands to her head to try and stop everything from twirling around.

Slowly Katie made out some small shapes in front of her. *My horse statues!* She felt the soft bed beneath her and realized with a mixture of both joy and sadness, *I'm home!*

Quickly glancing around, she saw that everything in her

146

room was exactly the same as when she had left. She also noticed she was still wearing the jeans she'd last had on at the ranch. But amazingly, her blouse had changed back to the one she'd been wearing the day she was sucked into the book.

The book! Katie eagerly began scanning her room for it. *I know I was looking at it before I left,* she thought as she searched around her desk, then her bookshelf, then under her bed. But the paperback was nowhere to be found. *It's like it disappeared after I'd done my part in it.* "That's so weird," she muttered out loud.

"Katie—dinner!" called her mother's voice from the kitchen.

Questions instantly flooded Katie's mind. *Dinner? Haven't you missed me all these weeks? Don't you wonder where I've been?*

"Have you washed your hands yet?"

Katie shook her head in bewilderment. This was definitely strange. Hadn't her mom even noticed she'd been gone?

Walking toward the bathroom, Katie looked down at her palms and saw several of Tango's reddish-brown hairs stuck there. Another lump started to rise in her throat, but she didn't get to reminisce long. Her brothers' bedroom door suddenly shot open and they both emerged, laughing over something that had just happened during their computer game.

"But his saber got that knight! I *know* it!" Mark said, imitating a sword fight as he stepped around Katie to get into the bathroom.

"No way!" Dave exclaimed. "You're just trying to claim you won when you didn't!" He gave Mark a playful shove.

Katie followed them into the bathroom and silently watched Mark turn on the faucet while he and his brother continued their argument. When Dave challenged Mark to a rematch, they both turned and disappeared back into their room again.

Katie frowned as she looked at her reflection in the bathroom mirror. *Hasn't **anyone** missed me?*

She glanced down and saw the tap water Mark had left running. At that moment she heard Zack's voice in her head saying, "Some people waste water and don't realize its incredible value. But without it, this ranch couldn't exist." She felt a stab of pain in her heart at the memory of his voice.

Katie quickly turned her attention back to the tap. "Hey!" she yelled toward her brothers' room, "we should turn the water off when we're not using it!"

Mark's head poked out his doorway. "Huh?" he said, looking annoyed. Then he shook his head, muttered, "Little sisters," and disappeared again.

"They need a trip to the ranch," Katie mumbled as she washed her hands and turned off the faucet.

In a few minutes, each member of the Carlson family appeared from various parts of the house and sat down around their dining table. The large pan of steaming lasagna made Katie's mouth water. "Yum! My favorite!" she said. "I haven't had lasagna in weeks!"

Every head immediately jerked toward her. Dave then looked at his mother and joked, "Well, Mom, I'm afraid that doesn't say much for your cooking when Katie can't remember she ate your lasagna last night!"

Deborah Carlson chuckled. "I guess not," she said good-naturedly. Katie swallowed hard and turned to face her mom.

"Honey," Mrs. Carlson said, sounding perplexed, "these are leftovers from dinner last night, remember?"

Katie's mind spun. *I've been at the Cassidy Ranch for weeks, but...*her eyes grew wide...*time here at home must have been standing still!*

Realizing that everyone was staring at her, Katie knew she needed to say something. "Of course, Mom," she giggled weakly. "I was just so excited about your lasagna again, I forgot for a second."

"That's okay, sweetheart. We all forget things," her mother said, glancing toward her husband with a twinkle in her eye. "One time your father forgot our anniversary."

Richard Carlson grinned and quickly held up his arms to defend himself. "Yes, but never again!" he said. "Believe me, *never* again!"

As they all laughed, Katie looked around the table at her family. A smile spread across her face as she thought, *I really loved the Cassidys...but it's awfully good to be home.*

Mrs. Carlson picked up a spatula and reached over for Katie's plate. Katie's heart began to pound a little harder as she realized an important moment had come. In a soft voice she said, "Maybe we should thank God before we eat." She glanced around, bracing herself for their reactions.

But dead silence followed as everyone stared at her again. Her father broke the awkward moment. "Well, Katie," he said with a puzzled expression, "how about you doing that for us?"

"Okay, Dad," she said. For an instant, the memory of her first meal at the Cassidy's table flashed through her mind, when she had been reaching for the food, only to freeze in mid-air. So she knew how her family must be feeling right now.

As Katie bowed her head, she saw Mark out of the corner of her eye, looking at her suspiciously. She clamped her eyes shut and said, "Thanks, God, for this wonderful lasagna. I love lasagna! And thanks for my family. I've learned how much they mean to me. And thanks *so much* for special friends you give us. Uh…amen."

"Amen," echoed her mother softly, turning to look into her daughter's eyes. An unspoken understanding passed between them in one of those special mother-daughter connections, and Katie sensed that her mom somehow knew something was different.

"So," her dad said, "when did you start thinking about God and religion, Katie?"

Katie knew that voice. It really meant, *I'm looking for some information here.* "Well…" she hesitated while gathering her courage, "I don't really know much about religion, Dad. But I…I asked Jesus to pay for my sins and mistakes and to come into my life."

At the mention of sins in her life, Katie saw both her brothers' heads come up at the same time. But her mom's piercing glance kept them silent. Her mother then smiled encouragingly at her and said, "Well, honey, I think that's great. I'd like to hear more about this sometime."

Her father, however, seemed interested in getting some answers right now. "Katie, how did you learn about all this?" he asked with a frown.

Katie felt a flash of panic. *What do I say? It's another one of those questions I can't really answer! They'd think I was crazy if I told them about the ranch!*

As her mind raced, the answer suddenly occurred to her. *Of course!* Calmly she replied, "It's all in the Bible, Dad." Then she quickly focused on her lasagna, as if nothing unusual had happened.

But her dad didn't seem quite satisfied yet. "Honey," he said, "you don't have a Bible, do you?"

At that instant, Katie remembered the gift Mrs. Cassidy had given her. But was it possible to bring something back from the ranch into her world? Katie quickly reached around to the back of her jeans—and found the small Bible in her pocket! She exhaled with relief and carefully drew it out. Holding up the beautiful little book, she said, "Yes I do, Dad."

Her father glanced at the small leather volume, and in a tone that betrayed his continuing confusion simply said, "Oh."

As the conversation around the table turned to other subjects, Katie was frequently aware of her parents' surprised expressions when she refused to get into arguments with her brothers. And when she even complimented Mark once, it came as such a shock to him that he didn't know how to respond! Katie smiled to herself, sure that her parents must be totally puzzled by the obvious changes in her.

After dinner, Katie retreated to her bedroom, thankful

for the opportunity to finally be alone. As she sat down on her bed, her eyes once again fell on the horse statues. Tears started to form as she reached down and lovingly picked up the chestnut stallion that looked so much like Tango. "I miss you, Tango," she whispered softly.

But the tears didn't come. Instead, happiness flooded her heart as she pictured Anna proudly riding her horse, thrilled at the chance to be outdoors and free from her wheelchair prison. A smile crept across Katie's face as she marveled at how it actually felt *good* to have given up what she wanted more than anything in the world for someone who truly needed it. *How weird!* she thought, shaking her head. *Giving up something can actually be better than hanging on to it for yourself!*

Katie gently placed the statue on her desk and sat down on her bed again. As she leaned back, she suddenly felt the small bulge in her hind pocket. *My Bible!*

Pulling the special gift out again, Katie ran her hand over the smooth leather. As she opened the front cover, her eyes fell on an inscription written in a neat, motherly hand: "To our sweet Katie—Wherever you may be, you'll always be part of our family. We love you!"

Once again, a huge lump formed in Katie's throat as she looked at each individual signature: "Matthew Cassidy, Mom Cassidy, Your sister Anna."

But when she read the last signature, tears finally did run down her cheeks. In a rough boyish scrawl were the words, "Your forever best friend, Zack."

Katie carefully set the small Bible on her desk beside the

horse statue and let the tears flow. Although her time at the ranch with the Cassidys had come to an end, she knew she'd always keep those precious friendships and memories in her heart.

With a long sigh, Katie dried her eyes and lay back on her bed. So much had happened! She wondered if life here at home would seem sort of dull compared with all the excitement she'd just had. Would she feel restless for the remainder of the summer, or would she be able to enjoy reading stories about other people's adventures again? One thing she knew for sure—she would definitely miss Zack!

But she wouldn't have worried about life being boring if she had known what was about to happen—and who would be going with her....

Before you close this book: ☺

While Katie is at Cassidy Ranch, she makes the most important decision of her life—she receives Jesus' payment for her sins so she can live with Him forever. Have you ever made that decision? If not, you could do that right now. You can pray along with Katie:

> "Dear Jesus, I *do* believe in You, and I thank You for Your offer to pay the penalty for all my sins and mistakes. I know I do lots of stuff I shouldn't, so I receive Your payment for all those things. And I ask You to come into my life so I can be with You forever."

The Bible tells us, "And this is what God has testified: He has given us eternal life, and this life is in his Son. So whoever has God's Son has life" (1 John 5:11-12). According to God's promise in that verse, if you have received God's gift of His Son (Jesus) into your life, you have eternal life. And eternal life with God and Jesus lasts for—eternity!

If you just prayed this prayer, why not tell someone? It's the most important decision you will ever make!

Blessings on you as you start this new adventure with Christ, Judy Starr & Katie Carlson

For more information about other Katie Carlson adventures, see **www.katiecarlsonbooks.com**

FOR THOUGHT AND DISCUSSION

Chapter 1

1. Katie loves to read, and her favorite book is about a ranch with horses, tall trees, and a red-roofed barn. What is your favorite book? What are some reasons you like it?

2. Katie is getting to fulfill a lifelong dream by suddenly winding up at Cassidy Ranch. What are some things you dream about doing?

Chapter 2

1. When Katie was alone in her room at the ranch house, she thought about how she'd never really had to share things before, and how she liked not sharing. What are some ways you act selfishly and don't want to share?

2. Little Anna said to her father, "I'd love to see Katie ride Tango... but only if she wants to right now." What kind of attitude is Anna demonstrating?

Chapter 3

1. Some people can become angry and bitter when they face difficulties. Even though Anna has a severe physical limitation, why do you think she responds so well?

2. How do you usually respond when you have problems?

Chapter 4

1. What has happened in Roberto's life because of his choice to rebel against his parents and run away?

2. How do you think Roberto's actions made his parents feel?

Chapter 5

1. Katie thinks Tango is hers, then learns from Mr. Gateman that she is there to calm the horse down so Anna can ride him. How does she react? What attitude is Katie demonstrating?

2. Should Katie have a different response, and if so, what should it be?

Chapter 6

1. Katie finds herself drawn toward Anna's sweet spirit. Yet Katie is also becoming very attached to Tango, and whispers to the horse, "I'm not even sure Anna should ride you." Why does Katie say that?

2. When they saw the mountain lion tracks, Katie didn't listen to Zack's advice to ride away from the tree and into the sunlight. What happened because of that?

Chapter 7

1. What does Antonia immediately do when she sees Roberto? How do you respond when you see someone who has been hurt or injured?

2. While sitting in the bunkhouse, Roberto thinks about the temptations that had looked so incredibly good to him, yet how they had turned out to be so terrible. What are some temptations you face that would be bad for you and for others if you gave in to them?

Chapter 8

1. Why do you think the Cassidy family, Diego, and Maria talk to God about so many things?

2. What kinds of things would you like to talk to God about?

Chapter 9
1. When Mrs. Cassidy talked to Katie about the Bible, she said, "Whatever God says to us, we can always trust to be right." Therefore, where should we always go to find answers to all our questions and problems?

2. Mrs. Cassidy told Katie about Jesus' incredible offer to pay the penalty for our sins. What does that mean?

Chapter 10
1. Katie makes the most important decision of her life when she receives Jesus' payment for her sins so that she can live with Him forever. Why is that decision also the most important decision of your life? Have you ever made that decision? If not, why not do that right now? (Turn back to page 105.)

2. After Katie received Jesus' payment for her sins, she noticed a change inside her. What was different?

Chapter 11
1. What is the attitude of Roberto's heart toward his boss, Jeremiah Parker?

2. What does that attitude make Roberto want to do? Is that good? Why or why not?

Chapter 12
1. Mr. Gateman tells Katie that in order to experience other great adventures, she must make the right choice here at the ranch. What is the choice now facing Katie?

2. Katie told Tango earlier that she didn't want to give him up and return home. What would be some results of that decision?

Chapter 13

1. Diego and Maria could have been very angry with their son for the choices he'd made. How did they choose to respond instead?

2. How did their actions then affect Roberto's attitude toward Jeremiah Parker?

Chapter 14

1. When Katie first arrived at the ranch, she thought that being selfish was okay. What big change has happened in her heart?

2. How does that change affect her actions and choices?

Chapter 15

1. The Bible tells us we become "new creations" when Christ is living within us. (See 2 Corinthians 5:17.) For Katie, what difference does having Christ in her life make in the way she now treats her brothers?

2. What are some things you have learned from this book that will make a difference in your life?

Turn the page for a sneak peek into Katie's next adventure:

Katie Carlson Adventure Series

ADVENTURE IN THE BAHAMAS

Judy Starr

CHAPTER 1

"Stop it!" Katie yelled as she slammed the door of her room in Mark's face and burst into tears. Crossing the room, she flung herself down on the bed and quickly buried her face in a pillow to keep her older brother from hearing her cry.

"Christian Kate, Christian Kate," Mark's taunts continued through the door.

"Mark…" Katie heard her mother's voice. With one word her mother could convey so much. "Come here, Mark."

Katie lifted her head out of the pillow to hear their footsteps retreating down the hall. Slowly sitting up on the side of her bed, Katie swiped her hand across her wet eyes. *I wish I was back at Cassidy Ranch,* she thought as she looked over at the dark chestnut horse statue prancing on the pink carpet. A sigh escaped from her lips.

For what seemed like a long time, she sat sniffling and staring at her statue. A soft knock on the door startled her. "Yes?" she said.

"Can I come in?" came her mother's soothing voice.

"Okay."

Her mom's sweet smile and sympathetic eyes instantly made Katie feel a little better—but it couldn't erase her anger. "I hate him," she mumbled, looking down at the floor.

Deborah Carlson sat on the bed next to Katie and wrapped her arms around the girl. "I've had a talk with Mark, sweetie. He won't tease you about your new interest in spiritual things anymore. I think he's just puzzled by the wonderful change we've all seen in you these last few days. But he won't tease you again."

Katie leaned her wet cheek against her mom's shoulder and sighed again. "I know I'm supposed to love him—but I *don't*."

Mrs. Carlson gave Katie a squeeze and said, "I think he's sorry, honey."

"Yeah, right," Katie muttered as she pulled away from her mom a little.

For a few moments the only sound in the room was the soft rhythmic ticking of the desk clock beside the bed. Finally Mrs. Carlson patted Katie's leg. "Why don't you go for a swim? That should make you feel better."

"Well, maybe," Katie said slowly. *Although that doesn't sound particularly fun right now,* she thought, *unless I could drown Mark.*

"It's beautiful today," her mom said, rising to leave, "and

I know you'll feel better if you just get outside."

"All right," Katie said as her mom swung the door shut behind her. Katie rose to change into her swimsuit, but she wasn't at all convinced that going swimming would help anything.

Pulling on her pink swimsuit, Katie kept thinking about how life just hadn't seemed right since returning from her adventures at Cassidy Ranch. She missed the Cassidys—and especially Zack. "Life here in Oklahoma isn't *anything* like riding Tango across the fields in Colorado," she said longingly. Hardly a moment went by when she wasn't thinking about her amazing time at the ranch.

A forceful knock on the door made her jump. She could tell it wasn't her mom. Katie knew her dad was at work and that her oldest brother, Dave, was at some club meeting…so that meant it could only be one person. "Go away!" she hollered.

"Katie, I'm…uh…I'm sorry about teasing you," Mark said.

"No you're not. Go away!"

There was a moment of silence, then she heard him mumble, "Well, I guess that religion stuff didn't change you after all."

As Mark's footsteps faded from her hearing, Katie tugged at her swimsuit and thought, *I wish I were an only child.*

Katie pedaled her bike through the city's side streets to reach the community pool, then securely locked the bike to a rack. She paid the attendant at the entrance, walked into the pool area, and stopped short. *That's so weird!* she thought, looking around. *There's no one here but the lifeguard.*

Spreading her big Hawaiian-flowered towel on the hard cement near the water's edge, she sat down and tied her auburn hair with an elastic band. Easing into the pool, her body began to relax in the warm water as she floated lazily on her back. *But I still miss the ranch.*

Katie squinted up at a puffy cloud hanging overhead. *Hey, that big ol' cloud looks sorta like Mr. Gateman,* she thought, remembering the man who claimed to work for the One who had somehow transported her through space and given her the ability to ride and rope like a pro. Just thinking about him made a smile cross her face.

"Hello, little lady," she heard someone say.

Oh great. Now I'm even hearing voices from the ranch, she thought, flipping over so she could look around. She peered toward the chain link fence on the opposite side of the pool, but the sun blinded her.

"Can't believe your eyes?" came the voice again.

Katie swam hesitantly toward the fence as she tried to figure out who was talking to her. Suddenly she gasped! There stood a large man wearing a straw Panama hat. "Mr. Gateman! It *is* you!"

Scrambling out of the pool, Katie rushed over to the fence. Instantly she felt the way she always felt around him—*small.* It wasn't just his huge frame that made her feel that way, but more his imposing presence which radiated power and importance. Yet he'd always been gentle and kind. "I'm so glad to see you!" she said, wrapping her fingers around the fence between them.

"Hello, Katie," Mr. Gateman said, his dark eyes meeting

hers.

Mr. Gateman's deep voice felt like a warm shower over her. "What are you doing here?" she said. "How did you get here? Do I get to go back and see the Cassidys?" she asked in rapid fire.

Mr. Gateman chuckled. "To which question do you really want an answer?" he said with a twinkle in his eye. Then his face became more serious. "No, Katie, you can't go back to Cassidy Ranch. Remember, we talked about that."

Katie dropped her eyes. "Yeah, I remember."

"But," he continued, "you are about to help someone else, and make a huge difference in quite a few people's lives."

"Huh?" Katie looked back up. "What do you mean?" As soon as the question was out of her mouth, she remembered how he never gave her answers—just more questions. But she thought she'd keep trying anyway. "What people?"

Mr. Gateman paused for a moment before saying, "Katie, what is about to happen may seem like a challenge at times, but you must apply what you're going to learn *there* to life *here*, because that will make a difference as well."

Katie frowned. "Mr. Gateman, I don't know what you're talking about," she said, shaking her head.

The large man broke into a huge grin and laughed. "You're a joy, Katie. You really are a joy," he said. "You make my job a lot of fun." Then his eyes bore into hers, and she remembered how it often felt as if he could read her mind. "Just be sure you learn what you need to and bring it back with you, okay?"

Katie's frown increased as she tried to figure out what on

earth he was talking about. "Learn what? Learn something here?" she said, looking back at the pool as she gestured toward it. "What am I supposed to—" Katie stopped midsentence as she turned back toward Mr. Gateman. Once again, he had vanished.

"How does he do that?" she said, looking up and down the fence. But he was nowhere in sight.

Slowly Katie walked toward the pool. *Now even the lifeguard has disappeared,* she noticed. *Strange things always seem to happen when Mr. Gateman shows up.*

Stepping onto the diving board, she performed a perfect swan dive into the water. As she paddled back toward the side, she continually replayed their conversation in her mind. *He said I'm about to make a big difference in some people's lives. Who? Maybe I'm going to kill Mark!* she thought with a grin. *And I'm supposed to learn something to apply here, he said. What does **that** mean?*

Katie's thoughts were interrupted when she spied a shiny object down by the drain hole. *Money! People are always losing coins in the pool.* She took a deep breath, kicked her legs above the water, and dove down. But an odd thing began to happen. Usually the deeper she descended, the harder it was to swim. But now it almost felt as if something was gently pulling her down.

Katie neared the shimmering coin beside the pool's small drain hole and reached out to pick it up. But instead, something pulled her arm over toward the drain…and actually sucked her hand *into* the hole! In a panic she realized, *My **entire body** is being pulled into this tiny drain!*

Instantly, Katie was stretched like a rubber band, long

6

and thin, as she slid through the impossibly small opening. *Help!* she cried silently. Then, in the blink of an eye, she popped back up to the surface, like a cork being released underwater.

Katie gasped for breath, more out of fright than from needing air. Adrenaline surged through her body like a blast from a fire hose. As she inhaled deeply, a small wave of water smacked her on the side of the face. Katie swallowed, then gagged and coughed. *It's **salt**water! Where am I?*

Kicking her legs to raise herself up a little higher, she looked around and saw miles of blue water in every direction. An island sat in the distance to her right, and another one behind her. A rush of fear swept through her—*I'm in the ocean!*

As she treaded water Katie thought frantically, *Can I possibly reach one of those islands?* But before she could make any decision, she spied something big and dark in the clear water just below her—and it was quickly coming toward her! She didn't have time to swim away or even scream before it surfaced right beside her!

THANKS

Thanks, first, to my wonderful husband, **Stottler**. You patiently encouraged me and reread this story throughout its entire process, always believing in me and in the potential of the Katie Carlson series. This book, and all the ones to follow, would have never happened without you! I love you *so much*!

Thanks to my brother, **Steve Antosh**. After Stottler, you were the first to read the original opening chapters, and then the first draft. Your encouragement really helped bring this book to life. Thanks!

And to all you girls who read the original story, you also contributed to it becoming a reality. Thanks **Kelsey Bruce**, **Jessica Elliff**, **Bree Jordan**, **Molly McGuckin**, **Sarah McLeod**, **Erin Opray**, and especially my niece, **Catherine Antosh**. And a special mention to **Piper Brown**—your enthusiasm for this book has given me much joy and spurred me on many times.

Also **Elsa** and **Abigail Schweizer**, and **Oliver Schumacher**, I greatly appreciate your help in making Katie and Zack real.

Thanks to my friends who read the first draft as well: **Pat Peterson**, **Nicole McLeod**, **Nietzie Toothaker**, and **Holly Elliff**. And to my dearest friend, **Bonnie Lang**, a special thank you for your love and encouragement that never fails.

Thanks, **Angel** and **Ruby Crosthwaite**, for giving me the opportunity to experience ranching life at Rancho Mission Viejo, and for answering my numerous questions so I could make this story as realistic as possible.

The names of my wonderful prayer team are far too

.umerous to write, but I have no doubt that because you prayed, this story has finally become a printed book. Thank you a million times for all your prayers!

David Orris, thank you for all your wisdom and counsel. You have been such a wonderful friend to Stottler and me.

Thank you, **Dave Koechel**, for all your help and for introducing me to **Carol Johnson**. Carol, I so appreciate you! Your patient mentoring and guidance has taught me so much! You are a fabulous editor, and I feel privileged to have gotten to work with you.

Barb Lilland, thank you for your "final hour" wisdom and input as well.

And **Chris Beatrice**, thanks over and over for your wonderful art, and equally, for being such a great guy to work with. As Stottler says, "You're a prince of a fellow!"

I've saved the most important for last. Thanks and praise to my precious **Lord Jesus Christ**. You guided me daily and gave me ideas, words, motivation, diligence, and perseverance. I know that apart from You, I can do nothing (John 15:5), so I give You all the glory, and say, "Thank You" with all my heart!